ODYSSEY
OF A
QUIET MAN

ODYSSEY OF A QUIET MAN

BRIAN CRANE

Copyright © 2020 by Brian Crane.

ISBN:	Softcover	978-1-9845-9503-4
	eBook	978-1-9845-9502-7

All rights reserved. No part of this book may be reproduced or transmitted in any form or by any means, electronic or mechanical, including photocopying, recording, or by any information storage and retrieval system, without permission in writing from the copyright owner.

This is a work of fiction. Names, characters, places and incidents either are the product of the author's imagination or are used fictitiously, and any resemblance to any actual persons, living or dead, events, or locales is entirely coincidental.

Any people depicted in stock imagery provided by Getty Images are models, and such images are being used for illustrative purposes only.
Certain stock imagery © Getty Images.

Print information available on the last page.

Rev. date: 05/27/2020

To order additional copies of this book, contact:
Xlibris
800-056-3182
www.Xlibrispublishing.co.uk
Orders@Xlibrispublishing.co.uk

CONTENTS

1 .... Alone
3 .... Dedication
5 .... Preface

ODYSSEY OF A QUIET MAN.
Part One.
Charlie And Iris.

1	Siblings	1
2	Thorndykes	7
3	Zephaniah Peebles	16
4	Impulse	26
5	Iris	34
6	No Going Back	42

ODYSSEY OF A QUIET MAN.
Part Two.
The Quiet Man.

1	Platform 7	47
2	Alone	59
3	Oakshott Road	71
4	A Foot In The Door	77
5	Winds of Change	82
6	Duplicity	90
7	Harold Morris	96
8	The Fly Trap	104
9	The Leather Tool Bag	113
10	Man On A Mission	121
11	Shilling In The Slot	130
12	End Of The Line	145

ALONE

Alone.
And my thoughts move to the stranger deep inside,
I am adrift upon a sea of my own pride,
I am everyman so do not pass me by.

Alone.
Can I hold the time it takes to share a dream,
When I am free to be I'll always be the same,
In my sky the moon will always remain,

Alone............

Alone.
Where no eye betrays the doubts I feel in me,
For nothing ever is the way that it seems,
Is my destiny forever to be,

Alone............

from the album 'Coming Home.'
by Brian Crane.

DEDICATION

For Sue.

'And...in the shadows passing by,
I see some that I called friends.
Will they remember me as well,
As I remember them.'

              From the album 'Old Town'
                          by Brian Crane.

ODYSSEY OF A QUIET MAN.

Part One.   Part Two.
Charlie And Iris.   The Quiet Man.

PREFACE

'The weight of the cross that you bear is measured by the guilt in your heart.'

Having lived and worked in the areas mentioned in the two stories, over time the significance that those areas had on my life became more apparent to me. As a result I developed an interest in the history that they had to offer, not so much the recent past but the past which in itself was a period of transition, which not only had immense ramifications on the particular areas that I refer to in my stories, but that of England the country they are a part of.

So it was that I set out with the sole intention of using the history and conditions of specific periods in time to place my stories in, and the periods I refer to are from the late Victorian era, to the dawn of what is commonly accepted as the new Elizabethan.

Odyssey Of A Quiet Man therefore is two stories, with the first, 'Charlie and Iris' leading directly into the second 'The Quiet Man'. Two stories of ordinary, unimportant people finding their own paths through the difficulties of the times that they lived through, and yet, each having links, not only through blood but through the consequences that are dealt out by the inexorable hand of fate.

And through the stories I have endeavoured to look in depth at the inner workings of the characters involved, at their strengths and failings, at their motivations to survive the very real hardships and adversities of their periods in time. Periods in time that I feel their twenty first century descendants would be incapable of coping with, let alone fully appreciate the tenacity of spirit that their forebears must have possessed.

Therefore, I leave you to hopefully enjoy something that has given me a great deal of satisfaction in writing. And in so doing, I trust that the stories will at least provide the reader with a thought provoking experience, which will lead them to either question or endorse the actions of the characters and the subsequent outcomes.

****

ODYSSEY OF A QUIET MAN.

Part One.
CHARLIE AND IRIS.

i.
Siblings

It had been a chilly autumn night giving an indication of even chillier nights to come, but now as the sun rose higher in the sky it was beginning to draw off the frosty dew from the roofs of the houses all around in a hazy vapour, giving them a rather deceptively mystical appearance. And yet, in the dark, broody shadows of the streets below, even at this early hour on a Sunday morning there was activity all around as the inhabitants of Hockley, this suburb area of Birmingham woke up to the stark reality of once again surviving the hardships of another day in this late Victorian maelstrom of life.

For even on the Sabbath, the Lords day there were many that saw it as just a continuation of the rest of their week, a perpetuation of their toiling existence. And now their sombre, hunched over shapes shuffled along to their places of work, only to be followed much later in the day by the weary trudge back again as the light once more dimmed from the evening sky.

There was no reprieve, for them or for those that relied on them, the families who were left behind in the damp and squalor of the well regimented but filthy, rat infested, decease ridden back to back system of houses. The families with more children than the average low wage of a few shillings a week was capable of feeding and clothing. And with the rent man calling weekly without mercy for his share, life was always going to be miserable and seemingly never ending. For in the latter days of the nineteenth century this was the norm with little or no concern for the plight of the oppressed masses.

Charlie Wilmot sat on the wall that fronted the steps of the Hockley Methodist Chapel staring at the all too familiar scene before him, at the ever increasing flow of wretched forms with gaunt, expressionless faces, the clattering horse drawn wagons and drays and the trundling hand carts and barrows. And all with the constant smell of coal smoke from the thousands of hearths and stoves mixing with the ever present stench of foul drainage and filth as this dismal world reluctantly crawled back to life from the daunting candle lit embrace of the night. For this was a world that he knew all too well, a world that he identified with every time some sight, or sound, or odour chose to tease his senses, even though Birmingham was not his place of birth.

Had it only been three years ago he wistfully considered, since he had first found himself seated on this very wall that fronted the steps of the Hockley Methodist Chapel.

"Three years!" he mumbled under his breath.

And with this notion filtering into his mind, memories of who he was and where he came from began to take precedence in his thoughts.

Born in 1882 in Cradley Heath, eight or so miles west as the crow flies from where he was seated and once a quiet rural heath land with a sprinkling of small villages until the late 1700s, when coal began to be mined commercially. As a consequence, it was only a matter of a few decades later before that coal brought the steam powered Industrial Revolution sweeping into existence and expanded the area into a township with the resultant influx of deep pit collieries, blast furnaces, iron working foundries, stamping and rolling mills and even an abundance of brick making works and so much more. And with the well established plethora of small handmade nail and chain making workshops, this expansion ultimately led to Cradley Heath being merged into the midst of what came to be known as the Black Country.

However, it was those who were the wealthy owners and employers who were the ones who raked in the profits of this maturing period of industrial enterprise, albeit at the expense of those they employed who worked long hours, in hot, filthy, unhealthy conditions for pitifully meagre wages.

Thus, it was into this impoverished and forlorn environment that Charles Edward Wilmot first saw the light of day and from the very outset life was a struggle, not only for him but for his older brother Albert by six years and his sister Agnes by four years.

At the time that Charlie first appeared, it was his mother Ethel who was the sole 'bread winner' of the family. Looking much older than her years she worked hard in one of the small, swelteringly hot, chain making workshops, hand forging the chain links with a dozen or so other women. And all for a pittance wage of eleven shillings for a twelve hour, six day week, merely to place food on the table and to keep a roof over her family's rented two small rooms, one of which was the scullery cum kitchen with access to a communal back yard with a washroom, water pump and privy.

As a consequence, much was expected of each of her children to help sustain the family, which meant that when Charlie's elder brother Albert turned eight he found himself alongside his mother in the noise and heat of the chain maker's workshop, with the daily running of the Wilmot family home falling onto the slender shoulders of the six year old Agnes. In a way something positive came out of this arrangement, whereby a bond developed between Charlie and his older sister which he carried with him long after the family dissolved with each of the siblings going there own way.

With survival being the priority of the day, school for the severely low paid classes was not even a consideration, due entirely to the fact that as soon as a child became employable thoughts of education fell by the way side. However for the Wilmot family it was fortunate that this was catered for in the evenings by Mrs Daphne Cooper an ageing, widowed neighbour who undertook to teach the rudiments of reading and writing that she had picked up while working in service for some wealthy landowner or other and merely for a seat at the Wilmot's table. It was an arrangement that seemed to suit both households and one that gave each of the siblings an advantage later in life.

The father of this industrious little family was Josiah Wilmot and someone who was noticeable by his continued absences. And yet this was not so much out of choice but more of being a victim of circumstances. To save himself from the cruel judicial consequences of a life of petty crime born out of a means to survival, Josiah had finally come to his senses and realised that the path he was taking would inevitably lead to a life in prison or even worse. And so, leaving his young, sixteen year old sweetheart four months pregnant with their first child and with promises of returning soon he had joined the army.

But with the vastness of the British Empire it was not uncommon for members of its armed forces to be away for years on end. This situation had led to the Military dictating that permission was needed for its serving men to marry, although refusal was by far the more common outcome. The principle behind this was that it relieved the fighting man of the encumbrance and responsibility of wives and families at home.

Even so this did not deter Josiah from becoming a father for a second and even a third time after more of his infrequent visits to his home town. So it was that in 1882 Charlie had followed his brother and sister into the dismal, hard working and poorly paid world of Victorian England. And yet, the sad part for Charlie was that father and son never actually met.

It was less than three years after his youngest son's birth that Josiah was posted to the Sudan with his regiment of the Royal Sussex Infantry as part of the relief force to break through to General Gordon at the siege at Khartoum. However, just days before Khartoum was finally reached, Josiah was killed at the battle Abu Klea in January 1885.

Not many tears were shed when the news finally filtered through of Josiah's death some five months later, for it was felt that although it was sad that he had died, he had been so much of a non provider and stranger to his family his demise had no real effect on anyone. The fact was that even though Charlie was now deprived of even a faint memory of his father, his older siblings could count the fingers of one hand the amount of times they had actually set eyes on him in the whole of their own short lives.

Nevertheless, to a certain extent Josiah's death was something of a reprieve for Charlie's mother Ethel when considering the fact that she was now spared the possibilities of having a larger brood to support, for although her three children were dear to her, three were more than enough. She addressed this minor upset in her life with little change to the well developed fortitude that she had employed during the whole of her journey through courtship to marriage to widowhood, albeit a marriage that was devoid of any formalizing ceremony or certificate and which was a detail that she kept very close to her bosom, even to her own dying day.

In spite of that, she did spare a quiet prayer for the late father of her children at the Cradley Heath Baptist Chapel that she attended every Sunday morning without fail. Somehow, it was in the pews of that austere building that she was able to find the sense of peace and solace that her soul was so badly in need of. And it was also there that she managed to replenish the resilience of spirit to face all the trials and hardships of her own harsh, impoverished existence.

But hardship was a part of every moment of every day without variation or change. And it was constantly all around with certain images that remained in Charlie's memory all his life.

Instances like the time Charlie's neighbour, fourteen year old Nathan Perks was seen stealing a leg of pork meat from the front display trestle table of the butcher's shop of Mr Edward O'Sullivan. The young boy's father had died of consumption and his mother was close to her own end through the same debilitating illness, when in an attempt to feed his five younger siblings Nathan had decided to risk everything for the piece of meat. But Mr O'Sullivan never worried the authorities over petty pilferers when he had three hefty, well fed sons as his own private constabulary.

So it was that the three guardians of the butchers little enterprise gave chase and when they cornered the petrified and pleading for mercy young Nathan in the alleyway at the side of the Wilmot's house, they beat him to such a pitiful state that for the rest of his foreshortened life he was blind in one eye and relied on a flimsy wooden staff to support his frail, broken frame. The sad part was that the infant Charlie witnessed the whole of this horrific act of vindictive retribution in a dumbstruck state of innocent disbelief, causing the images to lie dormant in his mind until such time that they chose to resurface, unannounced on many a subsequent long sleepless night.

To compound on this traumatic experience, shortly after there was the incident of the Sykes family of Henry and Myra and their seven children being evicted and having the bailiffs throw all their meagre possessions onto the filthy cobbles outside the hovel they called home. This situation had been brought about through the accidental spillage of molten iron at the foundry where Mr Sykes was employed, with the terrible consequence being that his legs and feet had been drenched in the white hot liquid. Of course the owners would not accept responsibility or even offer compensation but it meant that Mr Sykes was now badly crippled, and not able to work he had lost his job. And with no money coming into the household and the little that Mrs

Sykes had managed to put aside now gone, the family was in desperate trouble and three weeks in arrears with the rent.

But the culmination to the eviction was to stun the whole street, the whole of the local community in fact. It was when the sickly, gaunt faced Henry Sykes finally emerged on two crudely made wooden crutches and stood weakly but defiantly propping himself up in the doorway of the house. For a few long moments he allowed his piercing glare to penetrate deep into the eyes of all those who had gathered to witness the little drama. Then, lifting his torment stricken face to the clouded heavens he quite calmly took a long bladed knife from the inside of his dirt stained shirt where it had been secreted and with a determined thrust he raised it high above his head like some medieval knight wielding a sword.

"Damn you!.....Damn you all!" he shouted hoarsely in an heart wrenching outburst of thriving despair. "I'll not be a burden on my family!"

With that he then placed the tarnished blade below his upturned chin and ignoring the cries and screams of his wife and children, and the confused murmurings from the cluster of bailiffs and inquisitive residents of the street, he very deliberately pulled the blade across his stretching throat, opening it up in a wide gash of gushing blood. And the once proud, hard working family man Mr Henry Sykes then slumped, gurgling and twitching to an awkward seated position in the spreading scarlet pool, as it covered the doorstep, the door and its frame.

At the time this happened Charlie was not quite four years old but he saw it all from across the street as he stood side by side with his older sister, firmly clutching her hand and sharing tears of mutual horror.

But the one abiding image that not only affected Charlie but the whole of the town's people of Cradley Heath was when one of the nearby pits suffered heavy flooding and ten miners and three young boys of seven and eight years of age, working at one of the coal faces were killed.

Although Charlie was not quite as old as the youngest victim, he was able to sense the enormous depth of sadness that seemed to exude from all around him as he stood with his sister Agnes in the drizzling rain outside the colliery gates. This was along with the gathered throng of teary eyed mothers and fathers, wives and children and all the others who knew or had ties with the miners and who anxiously waited for the names of those who had perished to be officially posted.

And then watching, in a silence that seemed to envelope the whole sad scene like some giant cocoon of shared empathy of the moment, as one by one in a morose, shuffling procession the shrouded bodies were stretchered through the motionless crowd, to be carried and then laid on the floor of a nearby Church Hall.

For Charlie these were just a few of the so many vivid and lasting impressions that would stay locked away in the sensitive side of his head for the rest of his life, but they were also experiences which seemed to unify the sense of oneness that existed between himself and Agnes. Something so intangible to the outsider but to the two children, even of such tender years, was so real.

ii.
Thorndykes

Charlie took in a deep, quenching breath as the long established images began to thankfully fade once more from his memory, thus bringing him back to the present with something of a chilly shudder. He looked around for a few moments from his seat on the wall that fronted the Hockley Methodist Chapel, pensively absorbing the complete sense of hopeless gloom he could discern in the dark despondent figures passing before him on this early Sunday morning. And as he did he was slowly able to relax his mind enough to allow his drifting recollections to gratefully meander beyond his early years and the distressing impressions that they always seemed to summon up, to the years that he could look back on in Cradley Heath with a certain fondness.

He began to recall how the days seemed to pass without much concern to anyone, with each day resembling the one before it without any significant difference, merely the thought that for one more day at least the Wilmot family had survived.

Even so, it could be argued that they fared slightly better than others in that oppressed and poverty stricken community. For the combined hard work of Ethel and then Albert and even Agnes when she became old enough to cope with the work in the chain makers workshop made it possible for the Wilmot family to feel a sense of buoyancy from their labours that was not felt by so many of their neighbours. Although when Charlie reached the age of eight, good fortune favoured him when he was given a job in the stables of Mr Samuel Thorndyke the Wheelwright.

His position of 'stable lad' was under the aging groom Mr Joseph Patterson who had gone to his employer Mr Samuel Thorndyke requesting a lad to not only train up to take over from him but to be responsible for the work that he was becoming less able to do. It was an indication of the esteem that he was held in that his request was instantly agreed to. The fact was that his employer had a deep respect for 'Old Joe' who had been with the firm since he was a lad under the founder, Mr Samuel Thorndyke the elder, over fifty years before.

However, at the time Charlie first went to work at Thorndykes he was unaware that Old Joe had, in much earlier days been a good friend and neighbour of his grandparents and had been affectionately known as 'uncle' by their children, which included Charlie's mother Ethel and her three brothers and one sister. And even though the subsequent years had seen the two families taking somewhat diverse paths, Old Joe had tended to keep a discreet but watchful eye over his friends eldest daughter and her children and when the opportunity had presented itself he had used his influence to help its youngest member into employment.

At the start the work was hard and heavy for an eight year old but it was only what was expected of a child in the latter years of the Victorian era. Although, it was with a sense of pride that Charlie was able to contribute the majority of his meagre wage of one shilling and sixpence a week into the family fund. And as the years passed by, Charlie seemed to drop into the role of stable lad as if he had been born to it, with the five horses and two ponies seeming to take to his gentle and compassionate manner from the very beginning. And over time Charlie derived great satisfaction in the knowledge that he had been able to win the trust of such beautiful animals.

But a person can become so preoccupied by the day to day routine of their own lives that what exists beyond that blinkered perspective tends to remain out of sight and therefore out of mind. And for

Charlie, this was definitely the case, as nothing beyond the care of the stables and its resident's ever seemed to encroach on him and his day to day routine, which he later came to think of as his 'pleasing duties' and never simply as work.

Nevertheless, time has the annoying habit of passing by unnoticed and for the young stable lad within that closeted framework the days easily matured into weeks and months and so on into years without any apparent change. Aside that is, for the fact that his weekly wage increased at fairly regular intervals to the princely sum of three shillings and four pence by the time he reached the age of twelve.

It is also a fact that nothing ever remains the same and it was in Charlie's thirteenth year, that change demanded that the boy should become a man. Although it is seldom that anyone is ever prepared when change indiscriminately turns your world upside down.

For Charlie this was when all the hard work that his mother Ethel had put into feeding and housing her family over the years finally took its toll. The sad, tired woman, worn out from the perpetual grinding toil and worry fell ill with a bronchial infection, probably caused by a combination of the dusty fumes and heat from the chain making workshop that she had breathed in for over twenty years and then by going from the hot dry atmosphere out into the cold, biting wintry night air. Whatever the reason her weakened and susceptible stamina had not the strength to prevent this from developing into pneumonia and then pleurisy and at the age of thirty five, Ethel passed painfully away.

And even though her death was a source of deep sorrow for the Wilmot children, the situation was made even worse by the fact that their beloved mother was given a paupers burial in an unmarked grave. The reason being that they could not raise the two pounds eighteen shillings for even a basic funeral with a headstone, having spent what little money they could put together on the doctor's visits and medicines during their mothers illness and which still left them with an outstanding debt of two shillings and five pence farthing.

However by cutting back and scrimping in every possible way, including food and even Albert forgoing his vice of tobacco for his clay pipe, they managed to clear the outstanding amount in less than a month.

Despite all that, there was one source of some consolation which did come their way. This was when Mr Adam Jennings the chain master of the workshop where Ethel's two elder children still worked, out of respect for his deceased employee, allowed Albert the tools and the time to make a cross out of wood, with his mother's name and dates burnt into it with a hot iron.

So it was that a few days after the funeral, in the early grey light of a winter's bone chill morning the three Wilmot children identified the mound of newly turned soil which indicated the sad final resting place of their mother. And in a quiet, private ceremony the simple wooden cross was carefully driven into the cold, hard, pitiless earth.

A gesture of love and respect you might say, and so it was, but equally it could also be seen as a somewhat woeful and insignificant epitaph on a life that had seen nothing but hardship and wretched toil from beginning to the very end.

Again it was at this moment of deep tragedy that seemed to draw Charlie and Agnes closer together. So many times over the years each had confided their inner most secrets and had derived comfort in the council that each was able to give to the other. It was also at this sad time that Charlie seemed to glean a certain easing of the loss he felt in his mother's death within the pages of her well thumbed bible, which was probably the most treasured of her so few personal belongings and which he had hidden away after her funeral. And it became something of a nightly ritual for Charlie to immerse himself in a chapter, whilst giving silent thanks to the now deceased Mrs Cooper for her very persuasive insistence on the need to be able to read and write.

Although for Albert, who had now matured into a rather aloof and single minded senior member of the Wilmot family, this tendency towards the emotional and sentimental was far below him. Even when he had been meticulously making the cross, and when he had forced it into the hard frozen ground of his mother's grave, he most certainly did not allow the true hurt that he was feeling deep within him to show. Throughout that whole period of his mother's illness and passing he had been painstakingly careful not to give way to anything but the phlegmatic composure and resolve that his younger brother and sister had come to expect from him.

As if to emphasise this outward image of the strength in his character, a mere six weeks following his mother's funeral he calmly announced that he was leaving, as he wanted to see more of the world other than the perpetual heat and grimy hardship that was his lot in life in the chain making workshop and all for a miserly few shillings a week.

"God knows!" he declared. "There must be summat more to livin' than what's 'ere!"

It seemed that all the goading by their neighbour Mrs Cooper had at least opened up a questioning outlook in Albert, which he was insistent on following. And so, on one cold winter's morning with a layer of freshly fallen snow carpeting the ground, he waved a good bye and with his few belongings wrapped up in a small bundle he strolled away whistling. It seemed he had taken the job he had been offered on a barge plying out of Dudley and along the canal that connected with the extensive nationwide inland waterway systems.

There is a saying that 'changes happen in threes' and so they did for Charlie. It was not long after the transitional period in the lives of the Wilmot children, of their mother's death and Albert leaving that Agnes spoke to Charlie of her intention to marry. Although, in many respects this did not come as a complete surprise to her younger brother, when he considered the amount of times he had detected sly glances, sweet smiles and not so secret Sunday afternoon rendezvous' in the park between his sister and Eli Jennings, the son of the chain master.

So it was that within a few weeks the two were married at Saint Lukes Church, but the day had a certain air of sorrow in it for both Agnes and Charlie at the thought of such a joyous occasion being marred by what was, to all intents and purposes the final fracture in the Wilmot family unit.

That said, it was not until Charlie was walking away through the churchyard after the ceremony that the full impact of his encroaching life alone finally began to seep into his consciousness. For at the age of thirteen, to face the world without the strong ties that had previously bonded the Wilmot family together seemed a very daunting proposition indeed. And to add to this sense of dread brought about by his deep rooted trepidations of a life without his mother and Agnes and even Albert, was the fact that the rented rooms that the Wilmot family had strived so hard to find the rent for each week had also gone, which meant that Charlie was now homeless.

It was as he stood midst the varied array of aging monuments and gravestones with these considerations permeating through his mind that a sudden conclusion also entered it to confound him even more. It was that nothing was forever, for as the world turns so does the life that we live and no matter how good or wretched is your existence within that world it can change in an instant, one way or the other, for good or bad or worse. An astute conclusion for a thirteen year old you might say but it was one that was formulated by living through such harsh and exceptionally desperate times.

And yet, it did change for Charlie, for it was Old Joe who came to the rescue by obtaining permission from Mr Thorndyke for 'the lad' to billet himself in the loft of the stables until he could find himself something more permanent.

In fact it seemed to be far more advantageous for Mr Thorndyke to have someone living over the stables that the arrangement somehow stayed in place indefinitely. And over time Charlie, with the help of Old Joe and his good wife Betsy made the small loft space into quite a homely bolt hole for the young stable lad, and for some unknown reason it remained rent free with no deduction to the small wage he earned each week. Although for Charlie the solitude and the comfort that his little space provided was something that he had never experienced before and something that came to be very precious to him.

So all in all, it appeared that each of the Wilmot children had, in their own way landed in a place that was not only conducive to a happier, healthier way of life, it also boded well for their individual passages into the future.

But even though Agnes seemed to slip quite comfortably into her new dutiful role of a wife, as well as working alongside her husband in the running of the chain making workshop, she did not forget the bond that existed between herself and her younger brother. Very often she found opportunities to visit Thorndyke's stables with some reason in mind, whereby she would bring small treats of cakes and fruit and other small gifts. And it was the measure of the man that she had married that this was done with his knowledge and approval.

Even so the brief intervals in time when Charlie entertained his older sister in his little loft space seemed to take on a special importance, for it was then that they could rekindle the bond that had been so vital to them in their early years, simply by the sharing of memories and tit bits of news from their own situations whilst sipping tea and eating the treats that Agnes had brought with her. So much was derived by each of the siblings in these little family gatherings that each came to respect the value of them in their own way.

It was during one of the little 'heart to hearts' that Agnes informed her brother that he was to become an uncle. The news obviously came as something of a shock to the young man but it also seemed to exemplify the sheer joy that he had come to feel about his life in general. Even so the only comment that he managed to bluster out as he exuberantly embraced his sister was......

"This would've made our mother so happy!"

However, it must not be misunderstood that whilst Charlie and indeed the majority of the population of these latter years of Victorian England extracted what pleasures and inklings of hope that may come their way, life was hard, very hard. And in its own way, so it was for Charlie with the constant tending of the horses and ponies, the clearing and cleaning of the stables that Mr Thorndyke or one of his two sons would inspect at regular but unannounced intervals and all the other 'pleasing duties' his position of stable lad entailed. As a result, his employers found very little wanting or to complain about with the way that Charlie conducted himself. And of course he was always under the very watchful scrutiny of Old Joe Patterson, who kept a very close eye on his willing and hard working apprentice.

For apart from all the daily, run of the mill chores and duties, it was Old Joe who taught Charlie to ride the horses in his care and how to drive and maintain the various carts and carriages that the stables had in its possession. It was he who taught Charlie the blacksmith skills to make the shoes for the horses and how to keep the hooves in good health. He also taught his enthusiastic pupil what signs to look for in the animals to indicate that they needed treatment and then what treatment to give and how to treat them. Not only was Old Joe a good teacher but in Charlie he not only found a very attentive and capable disciple, but someone he came to know and have complete trust in.

And whenever the opportunity presented itself Charlie would accompany his aging mentor on his numerous excursions with the wagon and pair to deliver various items from the main wheel making and repair workshop to customers, or to fetch and carry from the other outlets of Thorndyke's little empire. On occasions this meant taking a wagon to the canal dock at Dudley where sometimes he was able to exchange a brief wave and 'hello' with Albert his older brother, as he worked his barge either in the direction of Birmingham with its maze of canal links or as he disappeared down the canal tunnel that stretched for almost two miles under the town of Dudley towards Stourbridge and beyond.

And yet, it was the excursions to Cradley Heath railway station to collect or despatch parcels that Charlie looked forward to the most. For it had been on the very first trip, only days after starting at Thorndykes at the impressionable age of eight and seated on the plank of the wagon with the reins resting gingerly between his fingers as he quietly waited for Old Joe to come out of the parcels office, that something happened to completely alter the young boy's perspective of his life and its values. It was when an engine in the Great Western Railway deep green livery, hissing steam and billowing clouds of white smoke had pulled into the station with a string of cream and dark brown painted carriages in tow. And in that moment something had erupted inside the young Charlie, a passion for engines and the power of steam that would remain with him for the rest of his life.

Many times, hand in hand with his sister Agnes and before he had come to 'Thorndykes' to work, he had watched the squat, black shunting engines going about their donkey work, back and forth on the narrow gauge sidings and links that served the various foundries and colliers in the area. But it was not until that one brief sighting of the true power of the steam engine, when his senses had been so excited by what he was seeing and to such an extent as to leave him gawping in speechless wonderment, that the seeds of fascination were deeply sewn.

And so following that first short trip with Old Joe to the station, Charlie would grab at any excuse that presented itself or when his free time allowed, to take himself down and along the railway line embankment just to watch as the locomotives chuffed and puffed their clouds of steam and smoke on their journeys to here and there and far and wide.

Sometimes he would just sit with a copy of a railway timetable he had acquired from the local station master, totally enthralled by what he could see and hear and smell, sitting and watching with an inner excitement building up inside while he waited for the next scheduled train to come along. And often he would wonder where this fascination for the railway system and its engines had actually come from. For truly it was a fascination, but it had not been until that first visit to the station and the collection of the parcels, that the fire in him had been lit. Even so it was as he pondered on these rather diverse notions, that he also came to the conclusion that the future was looking towards steam and he also considered whether his future might lie in that direction also.

Although, out of necessity this deep seated obsession with steam was always kept at a discreet distance from Old Joe in their daily conversations, who tended to mistrust those things that he did not understand and always diverted the subjects around to the horses he had known and cared for and the days well before steam had made its appearance. And yet Charlie always listened with an absorbed and attentive ear at what Old Joe had to say about those times that seemed like another world altogether to the inquisitive young lad. Often he would sit engrossed in the colour and humour and emotion that the accounts and anecdotes conjured up in his mind, for if nothing else the old man's storytelling was nothing less than very entertaining.

But very little could diminish the passion and even the love that over the years Charlie developed for horses, those magnificent creatures he tended to so devotedly on a daily basis. For no matter what the weather was like or what the world beyond the stables was doing to itself, Charlie was always able to wake each morning on his straw palliasse, in his small but homely loft dwelling space, with a smile and a deep gratitude for his own good fortune. Each day was different and always with something new to learn from Old Joe, who he now considered to be more of a good friend than a superior. And it can also be said, that in the young man the aging groom and his wife Betsy had found the son, the child they had so sadly lost at birth.

For as each day passed, more and more Old Joe was able to stand back and allow his young pupil to work alone, yet never too far from his watchful and critical eye. But the eye was never jaundiced, for Old Joe saw so much of himself in the young man before him and this kept the old man's blood spiriting through his veins with a vitality that was decades younger than his years. So all in all, the young man and his mentor, over time nurtured such a strong affinity with each other that in effect it became far more important than each could understand or even admit to.

iii.
Zephaniah Peebles

And even though Charlie's days were dedicated to his 'pleasing duties' at Thorndykes, and what spare time he managed to allow himself taken up by watching the trains, there was one obligation that he endeavoured to keep and respect before anything else and that was to his Auntie Nora. Being his mother's younger sister he made it a sense of commitment to walk over to nearby Newtown to visit her at least one evening a week when his tasks at Thorndykes allowed. There to spend an hour or so with any small job she might need doing, or even to help out in contending with her brood of five children that were aged between four and ten.

Somehow his widowed Auntie Nora scraped a living, twelve hours a day, slaving away barefoot pressing the clay into the moulds at the nearby brickworks. And it was only by the few shillings that the job paid and the small amount that her eldest son Josh brought home from his job at a colliery that her family was able to survive.

It must be said that the colliery was not what Nora had wanted for her ten year old Josh, but she had reluctantly agreed to it out of the sheer necessity of the paltry wages he brought home and this was with her constant dread that the same fate might await him as that which had cruelly taken her late husband. For her dear Jack had worked at the local coal mine from the age of seven until his untimely death at the age of thirty one, caused by malnourishment and the constant inhaling of coal dust. And Nora had managed, along with her five children, to nurse her dying husband through the final, painful two months of his life without the loss of a single minute at the brickworks and without any outside help.

Even now, the sense of pride that had prevented her from accepting any money from her late sister's son in what she referred to as charity, still did not allow her to take any of Charlie's pitifully low wages that he would willingly offer during his visits.

Be that as it may, he always seemed to arrive with at least one of Betsy's freshly baked loaves of bread, or a few eggs from the handful of chickens she kept in her back yard. For like so many households in those poverty ridden days it was common practice for people to keep poultry and for some to even fatten pigs and geese, merely to supplement their diets. There were even occasions that Charlie would bring potatoes or other seasonal vegetables from the little plot that Old Joe worked at the rear of the stables, all of which were gratefully, if reluctantly accepted.

Furthermore, to ease his Auntie Nora's concern for her son Josh, Charlie had taken it upon himself to encourage his young cousin to visit him at the stables whenever the lad was able. It was soon very clear in the unflinching manner that Josh approached the horses and ponies that he had a certain flair and affinity with them, and over time he was even able to overcome Old Joe's somewhat censorious nature and obtain a kind of grudging approval. And it pleased Charlie that he was able to do something positive for his auntie, a woman he respected and in his own way he loved for just being his beloved mother's sister.

Although strangely, there was very little resemblance between the two, with his Auntie Nora's petite, almost fragile frame and pretty facial features that his Uncle Jack had loved so much and the hard, forthright brusqueness of her older sister. For he could still visualise his mothers firm, strong physique that had gone well with the heavy, demanding work she had endured in the chain making workshop and which had been epitomised by the calloused, burn scarred hands and grey lines of her face.

But there was one common thread that his Auntie Nora had shared with her older sister and that was the tenacity of their character, a steadfast stoicism to survive against the adversity that poverty sought to inflict on them. All of which was enriched by an unshakable loyalty to their families.

So for Charlie his life seemed to be well and truly pigeon holed for him. On the one hand he was able to follow his passion for the growing influence of steam and to fulfil his obligations to his Auntie Nora and on the other hand there was his love and devotion for the horses and ponies under his care at Thorndykes. And even if the work at the stables was demanding and sometimes hard, it did have a satisfaction to it that gave each day a purpose, a goal of achievement. This could simply be by knowing that the residents of the stables were well taken care of and that each one of them had come to know and trust their young handler.

And there was the valued friendship and respect that Charlie had developed between himself and Old Joe, who would often refer to his young pupil as the 'whippersnapper'. A term that he used affectionately rather than in any derogatory way but it illustrated the easy relationship that had grown up between the aging groom and the well placed, maturing young man.

For there was a mutual regard that spanned the gap in their years and which was evident in the relaxed approach of their conversations and the sharing of their own life experiences, when Charlie would sit enthralled by his mentors accounts of the 'old days' before industry and back to back housing had enveloped the rural nature of small villages and hamlets of the area. And then Old Joe would sit silent and dismayed at his apprentice stable lad's memories of a family struggling to survive on a few shillings a week earned through twelve hours a day of hard toil in the swelteringly hot chain makers workshop that always seemed to be endured in such a silent, matter of fact manner.

Old Joe was very aware of the conditions so many of the population of the times lived under, but to hear it spoken of with so much passion and intensity always brought the suspicion of a tear to the old eyes that thought they had seen everything. And it was in such moments that he counted his blessings, in that he had lived and worked his whole life in comparative security and for a family business that had appreciated his work and loyalty enough to promise that the small cottage that they had provided for himself and Betsy was to be theirs to live out their days in. Yes he had been very fortunate and he was equally thankful in that he had been able to pass on some of that good fortune to the boy who had become more like a son to him.

And so the next few years moved inexorably forward and saw Charlie reaching his sixteenth year with his weekly wage rising to four shillings and tuppence and with life seeming to be well planned out for him. More and more Old Joe resigned himself to his little plot behind the stables to leave the work and running of the stables to his more than capable assistant. This was with the full approval of their employers, who appreciated the fact that Charlie had become a very proficient rider and handler of the horses and driver of the various carts and carriages and had even delivered unaided, a foul to his favourite mare 'Nellie'. And secretly, Charlie seemed to thrive on this independence and responsibility.

However things were about to change again for Charlie and it was as a result of one impetuous and somewhat regretful action on his part.

Charlie had his days all so well structured that it allowed him short periods when Old Joe was able to merely oversee the comings and goings of the stables without too much flurry or interference. Sometimes this was with young Josh, his Auntie Nora's eldest son who now came to help out at every opportunity he could manage away from the colliery. The lad had developed a very real interest in the work and had endeared himself to Old Joe in a similar way as Charlie had.

And so it was in these moments that Charlie would either indulge his passion, other than for the horses by taking the pony and trap down to the railway station on some pretext of collecting or sending parcels. It was then that he would spend a precious half hour or so just watching and listening and smelling the whole wondrous world of the steam engines, before making his way back to Thorndykes with his mind and senses fully revitalised.

And of course there were the visits of his sister Agnes with her cakes and her expanding family to look forward to, or then again he would walk the mile or so to his Auntie Nora's house for his regular, dutiful visit.

It was a few months after his sixteenth birth day that he made such an early evening visit that in its way was to change his life, a visit that was somewhat out of his normal routine but which would put him in a position of arguably being in the right place at the right time, a coincidence maybe or even a stroke of fate.

Drawing close to Langford Terrace where his Auntie Nora rented her two rooms, he caught sight of a tallish, slender, weaselly looking man with black sideburns and drooping moustache coming out of the door to her house. He was dressed in a brown tweed suit, a brown rakishly perched billycock hat and red necktie, which he stood adjusting for a moment before strutting arrogantly away up the street with a black leather satchel in one hand and twirling a black, silver topped cane in the other.

Charlie knew instantly who the man was, it being Zephaniah Peebles, a man blessed with the biblical name of a prophet sacred to the scriptures of the old testament and the name given to him by his upstanding and pious parents. Zephaniah, whose prophecies spoke of the day of judgement and of doom as, 'The day of the Lords wrath,' which would bring with it 'a day of wasteness and destruction, a day of darkness and gloom' when 'their blood be poured out as dust, and their flesh as the dung.' And as a prophet, Zephaniah's writings dated back some six hundred years before the birth of Christ and yet his name had clearly been of such importance as to be chosen as an example and influential guide by caring parents for their adored only son.

Now as Charlie continued to watch the receding figure of Zephaniah Peebles, he found it easy to recall reading those damning prophecies in his nightly ritual of a chapter from his mother's bible. It was equally easy for him to quickly thread through the snippets of gossip that he had picked up from one source or other that directly concerned the cane swirling, flashy gent he was now coldly scrutinising.

And yet, somehow he could simply not come to terms with the fact that the person he was watching had been the child of hearsay and rumour, the child with such a venerable given name as Zephaniah, the child who had been lovingly ushered through a devout and religious upbringing, who had been destined to mature into a man in the service of the church and of God. And from there it should have been a natural progression for him to become the source of spiritual inspiration and guidance for any community he might choose to commit his life to.

But sadly, it seems that somewhere along the bumpy road to adulthood the wheels of morality, integrity, charity and humility had somehow fallen by the wayside and had been lost to Zephaniah Peebles forever.

However, what Charlie did know for certain was that everyone in the area now referred to this particular man merely as Zeph Peebles, the rent collector for the owners of the mass of terraced and back to back houses in the area. It was this devious, slippery creature's job to use whatever pressure was needed to extricate the correct amount each week from the meagre wages that the households earned and without fail. It was also common knowledge that he owned the pawn shops cum money lenders in nearby Netherton and Oldhill and even though Charlie had never actually met the man, his reputation was infamous amongst the local population as that of a truly nasty piece of work with diverse and devious connections and with his finger in many an illicit pie. Someone in fact, who was completely devoid of any measure of scruples or moral values whatsover and someone who would stop at nothing to get his own vile and evil way.

And even as Charlie peered from the shadows of the alleyway as Zeph Peebles swaggered self-importantly on his way, he was amazed that someone had not taken it upon themselves to alter this vermin's physical appearance once and for all. But as the rent collector reached the junction with Talbot Street he saw the reason why this had never happened. For there, lounging against the wall of a house he caught sight of the man he recognised as William Briggs, 'Wild Willie' as he was known, a local bare knuckle fighter with an unbeaten record and a truly feared, brutal reputation.

Something else that Charlie remembered hearing was that Zeph Peebles was not only Wild Willie's 'fight fixer' but he also employed the 'bruiser' and several others of his ilk to not only do all his dirty work but also as some kind of personal bodyguard, obviously aware that retribution could be lying in wait round every corner. Not so much for the rent money that Zeph Peebles carried in the leather satchel, but out of sheer vengeance on the black heart that beat without either mercy or compassion.

And as the two men met, the broad, forbidding figure of 'Wild Willie' stationed himself obediently a yard or so behind his master, like some large, slobbering bull mastiff and the two disappeared around the corner and out of sight.

As soon as Charlie was certain that the street was clear he quickly hurried to the door of his auntie's house and without waiting to knock, he burst in, but the sight that he was confronted by made him stop dead in his tracks. For squatting on the stone floor of the scullery, her face leaning for support against the cold, black, cast iron stove was his auntie, clutching the remnants of her torn blouse to her bare breast. Tears were still pouring over her red cheeks and her long dark brown hair, that was normally caught up into a tidy bun beneath a linen mop cap was now hanging down in unruly tatters.

Without a word being spoken, Charlie found a woollen shawl that he draped over his auntie's shoulders before gently lifting her to a nearby chair. After what seemed like a very long time she managed to compose herself and through her shaking and stuttering, Charlie was able to discover the whole despicable story.

Apparently, his auntie had got behind with her rent by two weeks because she had needed to pay for all the various medicines for little Amy, Nora's youngest daughter and Charlie's cousin. It had been the aging Mr Clarence Beddows, who owned the local pharmacist's shop who had attended virtually on a daily basis with a selection of his own patent mixtures to treat the weakly, sick child. Charlie had known that the three year old had been very ill with whooping cough and on his visits he had even managed to bring vegetables and some meat donated by Betsy to help make broth, but he had been totally unaware of the pressure that his Auntie Nora had been under with regards to the rent, such had been the pride of the woman.

However, the worrying and most disturbing part of his auntie's account was when she confided to Charlie that the previous week Zeph Peebles had said that she should not worry and that she could pay the deficit off a little at a time. But even Charlie knew that it would be impossible to try to catch up once a family got behind, simply because ever farthing of the pitiful wages that were brought into a household were spoken for and the rent collector would know this.

So it seemed that Zeph Peebles had altered his agreed payment scheme and had come for the full amount due on the rent and had been 'disappointed' that it had not been forthcoming, but if it was not paid in full the next time he called, Nora and her 'brats' would be out on the street the same day. However, there was an answer he had explained, and that was to pay it off in 'kind' and he had given her a sample of what that meant just minutes before, but with it falling just short of actual rape. It had been little Amy starting her uncontrollable rasping cough with the characteristic high pitched 'whoop' in the only other room that Nora was able to rent, that had been enough to make the rent collector release his unwanted attentions on the weaker woman. And with one last threat regarding the outstanding rent, he had made a hurried, if bad tempered exit.

It was fortunate that Josh, Nora's eldest son and his younger brother James were still at work and her daughter's Alice and Tilly were out of the house on an errand, so that they had not been witness to their mother's degrading humiliation. But maybe Zeph Peebles had somehow judged that Nora was likely to be alone in the house before making his degenerate advances, even though they had been thwarted. Now Nora's fear was that she would not be able to pay the whole back rent and her family would either be out on the street or she would be made to give herself to Zeph Peebles. But how long would that go on for.

And so quietly settling his Auntie Nora down as her children began to arrive home, Charlie took his leave and made his way very thoughtfully back through the narrow streets to Thorndykes. And over the ensuing days nothing else found a place in his deliberations, other than the mixing of the worry and concern for his Auntie Nora and a pounding anger that in its way was frightening him. This was something that he had never experienced before, this sense that all he wanted to do was to inflict as much damaging pain and injury on this detestable excuse for a human being as he could. But this was nothing more than lingering immaturity he concluded and he came to realise the futility of even thinking that he could possibly take on Zeph Peebles with 'Wild Willie' constantly hovering in his shadow.

Even so, he did realise that the most important thing to do was to make sure that the hold the rent collector had over his Auntie Nora was removed and the only way to achieve that was by visiting her before the deadline with the majority of his slim savings from beneath his straw palliasse. For the good fortune of living rent free above the stables meant that his meagre wages were just able to stretch to a few pennies each week being stowed away in his small canvas wallet.

So it was that the day before his Auntie's rent was due he made his way to Langford Terrace. And yet it was only with a flood of proud tears from his auntie and much insistence on Charlie's part that he finally managed to get her to accept the twelve shillings that she needed to clear her outstanding debt and bring her up to date.

Charlie walked away from his Auntie's house with a certain lift to his head and not a little sense of pride in his step at the thought that while he had been able to help her he had only done what his mother would have wanted him to do. And it was with this firm belief filling his mind that he continued to trace his way back through the oppressive warren of streets and alleyways in the direction of his own familiar home turf and his horses.

However, he was still fully occupied with all his brooding thoughts when he suddenly realised he had turned into Dawson Street with its several shops including a shoemakers, an ironmongers and even a public house, the Draymans.

But there was one other shop that instantly caught his eye and that was J Root the tobacconists, for standing outside was none other than the loathsome Zephaniah Peebles, talking with another brashly dressed individual, but more importantly was the absence of 'Wild Willie'.

Some strange instinct now took over and before Charlie knew what he was doing he had strolled as nonchalantly as possible along to the tobacconist's window and within a yard or so of the odious rent collector. However, now that Charlie was there he was in a quandary of what to do next, for the tingling in his fists were edging him to thrust them into the smirking, mustachioed face of Zeph Peebles but he was also aware of the consequences of such a rash action in broad daylight and with witnesses. Even so he was able to catch the latter part of the conversation....

"....a sweet, tasty little piece in Langford Terrace that I've bin' linin' up," Peebles boasted, "who's just ripe for the pickin'...... And tomorrow my old chum I shall be eatin' my fill."

He then delved into a graphic description of how he would allow young, 'fanciable' widows to run up back rent and then threaten them with eviction. After that it seems it was easy for him to 'take his pleasure any which way he wanted' until he found some other fresh meat, with the outcome being that the eviction would inevitably go ahead anyway.

Listening to this, Charlie's anger began to boil like a cauldron deep within him, for the mere mention of Langford Terrace had set the pulse pounding in his temples as his face began to flush and he quite literally was seeing red. But then to his left he sensed a large, imposing presence beside him and instantly he felt the futility of the moment, for there standing in the doorway of the tobacconist shop was 'Wild Willie', his battered face an indication of the battered brain that sat in confusion within that scarred, shaven skull. Far too many fights had left his thought and reasoning processes at a snail's pace but his brutal fighting instincts were known to be more than intact, and Charlie had heard more than enough to realise that he would be no match for this experienced and callous 'bruiser'.

Seeing that his bodyguard was again able to fill his clay pipe in the tobacconists, Zeph Peebles bid a farewell to his chatty acquaintance and strolled arrogantly off down the street followed by his obedient bloodhound. Charlie was now able to glance to his side and watch them go, confident in the knowledge that neither of them and especially 'Wild Willie' had taken the slightest interest in the 'boy' who had stood between them.

And even as Charlie continued to watch the two figures disappear from sight a fierce determination began to erupt within him, which caused his teeth to grind together in anger and his fists to open and close with such intensity that he felt his nails dig deep into his palms. For this was a new experience for him, this sense of sheer hatred and overwhelming need to inflict as much bodily damage onto that loathsome excuse for a human being as he could. And deep down he knew he was capable of doing it.

For no more was Charlie the little 'whippersnapper' but a strapping young man who thrived on a reasonably healthy diet and hard but invigorating work and the dark bleak days of his early youth on the streets had taught him how to take care of himself. And this ability had been augmented by the intense sparring in the back yard of their old house with his older brother Albert, who had taken a keen interest in the art of boxing, not only that which was governed by the 'Queensbury' rules but also that which he had referred to as 'back alley scrapping'. And Charlie had seen his brother settle a number of disputes in a very effective manner using these skills and which he had passed on to his younger brother, along with the knowledge of the places on the body that would cause the infinite amount of debilitating pain without too many visible signs.

Now Charlie was able to rationally peruse the problem that he was setting himself and he was able to come to one important conclusion. It was that Zeph Peebles probably had a set routine to his weekly rent collecting and so it would then be possible that he would be in this area around the same time each week. And with a smile beginning to adorn his face he walked calmly away from the tobacconist's window, whispering to himself......

"I'll be seeing you soon...Mr Zephaniah Peebles!"

Even so, the next day Charlie managed to elicit an hour so that he could watch from the shadows as Zeph Peebles entered his Auntie Nora's house and less than a minute later had come back out, fury written all over his face as he stormed up the street to be met and then followed by the ever present 'Wild Willie'. Obviously, the calculated attempt to get this 'sweet, tasty little piece' into debt and then into his control had been foiled and there was a certain satisfaction for Charlie as he turned away in the opposite direction, with an even firmer set to his jaw at the thought of what he was now committing himself to do.

iv.

Impulse

Charlie suddenly looked up as the loud clattering sound of a heavily laden dray passed close by, its two horses steaming and their hooves ringing on the cobbles with the weight of the load they were pulling. In the distance he could just make out the strident whistle and huff and puff of an engine on the GWR line out of Birmingham that led to all points west. All of which were mixing with the subdued murmurings of the steady flow of ragged shapes passing before him, all with a purpose to be somewhere on this early Sunday morning. Sounds that were all so commonplace to him, but sounds that had now jarred him out of his ponderous musings and back into the present, with him seated on the wall that fronted the steps to the Hockley Methodist Chapel.

He gave a cursory glance around at the wretched scene before him, at the grey houses and grey streets and the grey people with their grey faces and grey lives, where any kind of colour of any shade, or tone or tint was an exception rather than the rule. Where, he had somehow come to be accepted as one of these colourless and anonymous shapes that no one even noticed through the bleakness of their own desolate existences.

And he was just about to remind himself that even though it was three years since he had first found himself seated on this very wall, that he became aware of a tall figure in the uniform of the local beat bobby approaching on the other side of the street, while keeping rigidly to his two and half miles per hour authoritative gait. There would have been a time when Charlie had first arrived in this suburb part of Birmingham that he would have done everything to avoid the scrutiny of this imposing example of the constabulary. But today the staunch law enforcer, satisfied that Charlie was a familiar face, even at this early hour and not known for giving trouble, passed on by with the briefest nod of his helmeted head and without a glance back.

Even so it was enough for Charlie to once more delve back into his memories to dig out the unpleasant events that had brought him to this place, to this wall that had come to hold so much significance in his life. And thinking back, it all stemmed from the moment that he set his jaw to the task of dealing out retribution on Zeph Peebles, when nothing else seemed to matter to him. So much anger still seethed within him whenever he brought to mind the distressing sight of his Auntie Nora clutching her torn and bruised dignity close to her breast as she had tearfully described all that had happened to her.

Charlie now let his mind drift back over those disturbing thoughts and images which had churned inside his head constantly and without relief and which had stoked the fire that had been beyond extinguishing. For the mere fact that the slimy, slithery rent collector had actually laid his sticky hands on his mother's sister had been enough to set Charlie's dormant outrage ticking like some kind of vengeful time bomb. And with gritted teeth and fists performing a slow, rhythmic clenching and opening he began to relive that whole period of his impetuous, anger driven act of revenge

Following the chance encounter outside the tobacconists shop and at every opportunity that his employment would allow, Charlie managed to covertly track the movements of Zeph Peebles and the brutish Wild Willie Briggs. It was then that it became very clear to him that although he knew he was more than capable of tackling the rent collector he would be a fool to think that he could match the bare knuckles of his bodyguard, so he needed to formulate a plan that could possibly separate them, even momentarily and Charlie soon realised that greed would be his best ploy.

And on a Friday afternoon five weeks after the incident at his auntie's house Charlie found himself across the street from the tobacconists shop, his chosen venue for retribution.

From previous visits he had noticed a dark, narrow alleyway that led down the side of the shop to connect with the next street and a matter of only a few yards down the alley was a deep set side entrance doorway into the shop itself, which to Charlie's mind was the ideal place for what he had in mind.

Also, he had been able to confirm the exact pattern to Zeph Peebles route, with the rent collector arriving within twenty minutes or so at the same spot each Thursday. It also struck Charlie how strange it was that without any visible or audible signals the streets seemed to empty of people in anticipation of the grim reaper of rent, making his unwelcome appearance. And when each door was knocked, the transaction of the money being handed over and the ledger signed was swiftly undertaken and only when Zeph Peebles had moved on into the next street did the routine of the residents seem to trickle back to normal. Such was the sense of fear and foreboding that existed within the downtrodden and servile community.

Charlie was also able to confirm that Wild Willie invariably bought the evil smelling tobacco that he primed his clay pipe with at approximately the same time each week, so fitting nicely into the schedule of the rent collector's round. Nevertheless, the important fact to Charlie was that Zeph Peebles always waited for his bruiser to finish his business in the tobacconists while lingering at the entrance to the alleyway, and this was usually without anyone else about and for a period of no more than three to four minutes. It was this few minute's that the rent collector was without his ever present bloodhound in close attendance that was the final detail in Charlie's simple plan.

So moving casually to the top of the street, Charlie nonchalantly leant against a house wall with a full view down Prentice Row in the direction that he knew Zeph Peebles would be coming from. And to give a little more credence to his pose of the 'lounger' he pulled an apple from his coat pocket and began to take slow, methodical mouthfuls. However, he did not have to wait long for he caught sight of his quarry turning into the street, some eighty or so yards from where he was standing. For a matter of a few more seconds he watched Zeph Peebles arrogant approach, with his rent collector's heavy money satchel pressed tightly to his chest. And in his wake was the broad, bulky shape of Wild Willie, who even from a distance presented a formidable shadow behind his handler.

Without too much movement Charlie sidled back out of sight of the two figures and pulling his cap tight down over his forehead he approached the tobacconists shop and slipped unnoticed into the entrance to the alley and once inside the shadowy darkness he drew from his trouser pocket a small handful of coins. Choosing is one and only shiny silver florin he placed it temptingly just inside the alleyway entrance, just enough to be in full view of any passerby and hopefully this would be Zeph Peebles. The other coins, which included a couple of silver sixpences and several thrup'ny bits he placed at regular intervals to lead down into the darkness of the alleyway and so halt adjacent to the deep set doorway. Then pulling his scarf tightly around his face he stepped back into the dark recess and waited.

And he waited, as his mind imagined the rent collector's progress down the emptied streets, knocking on doors to complete the business of taking the hard earned shillings of the households, without any morsel of conscience or sympathy.

After what seemed like an age Charlie was just able to detect voices, the first was the rather nasally shrill tones of the rent collector himself and the other was the throaty grunt of Wild Willie, caused by the damage to his larynx, a consequence of the many fights he had fought. But then a brief silence descended, almost as if it was in expectation of what was to happen next. Even so, when Charlie finally heard the scrape of a shoe on the hard surface of the alleyway he could feel the hairs tingle on the back of his neck as his whole body tensed up ready to spring. His plan was working, greed and avarice for the shiny coins had sent caution flying into infinity as Zeph Peebles began to follow the money trail right down towards his waiting adversary.

A number of things seemed to happen all at once for the hated rent collector as he searched on the hard floor for any more loose coins that he may have missed. The first thing that he became aware of was a fleeting glimpse of a broad nebulous shape bearing down on him and the next was the fear as any cry for help was instantly thwarted by a tight grip that locked around his throat, forcing him backwards and up against the alley wall, even before the slightest squeal for help could leave his lips. And then the first crunching, sheering blow smashing into the centre of his face. The punch to the nose that Charlie had been taught to use by his brother Albert, that if swiftly and deftly delivered would have the most blinding, devastating effect on even the biggest bully thus rendering them to the mercy of whatever was to follow.

And what followed over the next ten seconds or so, as Charlie kept his victim suspended off the floor by means of his vice like grip around his throat, was the most vengeful pounding into the rent collector's body that Charlie's other fist could muster. And his final act before allowing the gasping almost semi conscious body to drop to the floor was a crashing knee into its twisting groin.

Charlie stood back for a moment and took great satisfaction at the sight of the groaning, badly bloodied heap at his feet. There was no sense of regret at his actions just an overwhelming release of all the anger and rage that he had carried with him over the last month or more. But he did feel a sense of justification of his actions when he thought of not only his Auntie Nora but all the other women who must have been subjected to the bullying and abusive attention of Zeph Peebles over the years. For another moment Charlie stared down unsympathetically at the grovelling, whimpering form, when suddenly he became aware of a throaty cry emanating from somewhere near to the doorway of the tobacconists shop.

"Mr Peebles sir!.....Mr Peebles!" came the urgent, almost unintelligible enquiry from a voice that was instantly recognisable to Charlie as belonging to the rent collector's absent bodyguard.

So it seemed that Wild Willie had purchased his tobacco and had noticed his master was missing, but his next move would most certainly be to look down the alleyway. So, quickly bending down Charlie retrieved his coins from his victim's trembling, clenched hand before turning smartly away down the alley in the opposite direction. And with a very satisfied smile adorning his face, he finally disappeared into the maze of streets of terraced houses that led, by a roundabout route back to his hidden refuge in the loft of Thorndykes stables.

Over the next few days the enormity of what he had actually done was brought home to Charlie. For now the thrill and the tension that had accompanied all the planning and thought that had led up to his attack on the rent collector was dampened to the point of being doused completely. News of the assault filtered through the whole community like wild fire, with so many not only saying that Peebles had only got what he deserved but were congratulating the anonymous assailants. Even Old Joe had voiced his admiration for those who had perpetrated the attack, but he also said that they should return the rent money to the poor devils that Peebles had taken it from, which in a way seemed to epitomise the innate honesty of the aging stableman.

Nevertheless that was the twist in the tail, for the official version taken from the badly injured rent collector's statement was that he had been attacked in the lawful execution of his duties by three anonymous footpads who had stolen his satchel containing the day's collection. And even though his assistant had tried bravely to intercede, the three attackers had been armed with cudgels and had been too much for him. Now Zeph Peebles employers were demanding from the police that all efforts should be made for the speedy apprehension of this gang of ruthless, armed robbers.

But the ensuing, intensive hue and cry caused by the pressure brought about by the wealthy, influential businessmen landlords, very soon changed when the stolen satchel and its contents were found in Peebles own rooms and as a result his whole account and statement fell flat. For now the police were looking for only one individual, who had been seen on a number of occasions lurking in the vicinity of the tobacconists shop, but the descriptions being given were all very vague and inconsistent.

In spite of this the respect of the community changed also to one of hero worship for the solitary man who had unselfishly put an end to the Zephaniah Peebles regime of terror, especially when this was endorsed with Peebles being charged with the theft of the rent money and with Wild Willie Briggs being implicated as his accomplice. And there was likely to be more charges to follow as Peebles whole method of working came under very close investigation.

Even so, all this was getting to be too much to bear for Charlie. In truth he had no regrets for what he done and equally there was the bonus to his actions in that Zeph Peebles and his dangerous crony Wild Willie would now be removed completely from the hard working community. And there was also the strange satisfaction that he had felt at seeing the result of his work lying at his feet in a cringing, bloodied mess.

However, the notoriety that all this produced was put into stark perspective as time went by. For all the initial excitement began to gradually drain away to leave Charlie with a gripping sense of guilt, especially when it became common knowledge that the police investigation had changed direction. The consequence of this on Charlie was that every time he stepped outside the boundaries of the stables he felt eyes were upon him and deep down he knew he could not live under that kind of scrutiny. Sooner or later, he kept thinking he would cross paths with someone who would recognise him and then the game would be up and it would not matter that the community in general felt the mysterious assailant on Zeph Peebles had done a worthwhile job, the fact was that it would still be a long prison sentence if he was caught.

It was almost a month to the day after Charlie had taken his law of revenge into his own hands that he finally confronted his conscience with a crucial and hard fought decision. It was that he could no longer wait to be arrested and that he must leave, but to where for Cradley Heath for all the good and the bad, for all the filth and the poverty was all that he knew, so where was he to go. But at the same time he remembered that his older brother Albert had taken the bull by the horns and from the occasions that he had seen him and even briefly spoken with him, he seemed quite happy with his choice. However, his brother did not have the threat of arrest hanging over his head.

The first person he confided in was his sister Agnes, when she made one of her welcome visits to the stables with her now growing brood of two. Although there were tears at hearing the full story and also her brother's decision to leave, she made it quite clear that she agreed with the consensus of opinion of the community in that 'the place was best rid of that kind of evil scum!'. Charlie's final gesture to his sister was to entrust their mothers rather worn and fragile bible into her safe keeping, saying that he did not want it to fall into the wrong hands.

Next it was with Old Joe over a flagon of the beer that Betsy brewed. Charlie had long come to consider the aging stable man as so much more than just his superior in the stables. And after a few moments of digesting the announcement, Old Joe quite calmly stated that it had not come as a shock for him to learn that the 'little whippersnapper' had certainly gained his respect and his spurs by championing his Auntie Nora's cause. However, he did express a deep sadness at Charlie's decision to leave but he understood, especially with what the consequences of remaining might be.

It was also decided that, with Mr Thorndykes approval Charlie's job should be taken over by Nora's eldest son Josh, who had shown such a growing interest and aptitude with the work in the stables on the occasions he had visited his cousin. It was also clear that the fatherly figure of Old Joe and even Betsy had taken to this other little 'whippersnapper' in a similar way as they had been taken with Charlie. And Old Joe had expressed his approval by saying that....

"If it keeps the young'un from a life down the pit....... then it must be a good thing."

So the die was set for Charlie and on one early morning a day or so after his conversation with Old Joe he packed his few belongings into a cloth bundle. And following a very tearful farewell to each one of the horses and ponies that he had grown so fond of he made his way, even as the dawn workers began to trundle there way down the streets towards their places of work, out into a future that appeared as dark and forbidding as the sky that he was walking under.

However, there was one final stop he needed to make and that was to his Auntie Nora's. Even at this early hour she had been up with some chore or other to help maintain the fabric of the pitiful two rooms she and her children lived in. Although she was surprised to see her nephew she was more than grateful at the news her son Josh was being offered a job at Thorndykes stables. And yet, she was truly dismayed to hear of the reasons why Charlie was leaving and shocked that it had been him who had taken it upon himself to 'sought out that devil's spawn Peebles'.

"And you did that for me?" she had questioned with a definite catch in her words.

But the only answer Charlie gave was to press three shiny shilling coins into the palm of her hand and to place a gentle affectionate kiss onto her cheek, before taking his leave.

v.
Iris

Further recollections were now beginning to become somewhat blurred in Charlie's mind as he continued to sit on the wall that fronted the steps of the Hockley Methodist Chapel. And struggle as he might he found it increasingly difficult to put the subsequent events into some kind of order, or to say for certain exactly where his tramping feet had taken him. Perhaps it was because he did not want to remember the details of that time when he put his life on hold whilst searching for something tangible to hold onto.

Be that as it may, certain images and impressions did seem to stand out a little clearer through the morass of muddy memories that his mind tended to evoke and some parts of that distressing period did surface for him to once more ponder over again.

After leaving his Auntie Nora's house his feet took him on an aimless trek to nowhere, with the first two nights seeing him sleeping with his belly empty under a canal bridge, before being forced to make a hurried escape from the clutches of a group of gypsies who wanted what coins he might have, plus the contents of his small bundle. But determination led him onwards along the canal trail before he found a day's work, unloading coal barges for a meal of cabbage soup and three pennies.

From there, it was a long daunting tramp from one place to the other, taking what work he could find on the way that might pay with a few coppers or maybe a frugal meal of bread and cheese or sometimes a bowl of warming soup. But invariably it always seemed to be work that rarely extended any further than a day or very occasionally two. So this meant that wherever he managed to lay his head he always woke with the same dilemma, that of finding something to ease the perpetual aches of hunger in his belly and work of some kind to carry him ever forward in the direction of what he was cynically coming to view as oblivion.

On the odd occasions when the weather took a serious turn for the worse and his funds could stretch to it, he would find shelter in one of those pits of despair, the 'dosshouse'. There for tuppence a night, he would be seated on a long bench, squashed between dozens of other homeless and lost souls, all leaning over the thick rope that was stretched tightly before them at chest height. Each one, for whatever reason seeking the dubious comfort of a dry night, albeit in the compressed, foul smelling and infested atmosphere that was the lowest possible refuge for the desperate.

Be that as it may there were a couple of occasions when he was able to secure himself the comparative luxury of a wooden cot and a hot meal at a 'Sally Army' shelter in Walsall. But the demand outstripped the places, so mostly it was sleeping rough anywhere that he could find which was secluded, reasonably dry and in particular, safe. The fact was that the small amount that had been left over from his meagre savings had soon been spent and so he was now totally reliant on the pennies he earned through odd days of work. However, work for his strangers face was very hard to come by with the local population in each area he came to being very possessive of the available positions on offer.

And so it was that the daunting prospect of life on the road, meandering from one desperate location to the next seemed to Charlie to be the price he must pay for his vigilante act against Zeph Peebles. If he had known how much he would give up by his rash, impulsive act then perhaps he would have chosen differently. But always there was the distraught and tearful image of his Auntie Nora with her blouse ripped open and only moments away from actual rape. And the really disturbing fact was that she could have expected little or no recourse from those in authority, for one of her lowly class. All this simply went to convince Charlie, even at his lowest of moments that he had done the right thing.

Nevertheless, he had now lost everything that his simple life had held dear, the horses and ponies, his homely loft hideaway and his hard working but satisfying existence with his good friends Joe and Betsy Patterson. But at least every day and every mile he tramped was another day and a mile away from arrest, conviction and a long prison sentence and for that he was very grateful.

But fate has a very determined way of finding a balance to certain events. And so it was that on one particular night and almost three months after leaving his home town of Cradley Heath, Charlie found himself a safe place to doss down in a tarpaulin covered goods wagon in some railway goods yard or other. Perhaps it was the attraction of being close to his other passion of steam engines that seemed to offer some kind of comfort to the growing fragility of his morale and self confidence, but Charlie was too exhausted and hungry after a long day of trudging around looking for work to allow himself the strength to even attempt to analyse any reason for his choice of billet. And soon it was sleep, a deep soundless, dreamless sleep that offered the only kind of solace that really mattered to him.

It was the banging and clanking of the goods wagons being shunted backwards and forwards that woke a very drowsy and confused Charlie. And as he peered from beneath the tarpaulin cover, out into the early morning gloom it came as something of a shock to him when he realised that he was certainly not in the same place as the one he gone to sleep in. Cautiously he vacated his overnight berth as quickly as he would dare, for fear of being discovered and soon found himself walking through a large cemetery before he came out into a maze of dark, dismal streets. It was there that he stopped to take stock of his surroundings.

"Where am I?" he asked himself, but no matter how hard he looked at his surroundings he could find no answer, no recognisable point of reference to build on. For even the smells of this place were different. Of course there was the burning coal and the sewage and the so familiar aroma of horses, but there was much more that remained anonymous to his nostrils.

Rather than wait in one place for it to look suspicious he began walking with his tired, heavy footsteps carrying him down street after dark depressing street, with the feeble glow of flickering candles desperately trying to illuminate the gloomy interiors of the waking houses as he passed. And as he passed along, with each street seemingly identical to the one he was turning out of, he was confronted with the ever daunting truth that this was another day that he must try to survive.

Occasionally he would halt for a few moments on street corners and gaze around bewildered, trying in vain to find something identifiable in what he could see, but in the slowly creeping light of the early Sunday morning there was nothing that was even vaguely familiar about his surroundings.

It was after perhaps an hour of wandering around, up one street and down another, as indistinct shapes began to spill out of the houses and onto the cobbles to begin their habitual trudge to their places of work, that Charlie finally came across a building that at least he had some kind of affinity with from those long lost years in Cradley Heath. It was a Methodist Chapel and with a feeling of muted gratitude at finding somewhere to belong, he sat down heavily on the wall that fronted the steps.

And seated there with the whole futility of his existence now weighing down on his shoulders, he gradually allowed his head to bow forward with a deep, despondent sigh that seemed to finally drain him of every last ounce of his diminished sense of determination and resolve. With an inward cry of despair ringing in his head he buried his face deep into his hands as a kaleidoscope of hazy images began to creep unannounced into his muzzy, befuddled mind. Images that were all without foundation or context, merely faces and places that melted one into the other, and which left him with a shudder of inner annoyance at not knowing what to feel anymore or even how to respond. And strangely, it seemed that he had very little control or even choice as to where his tumbling, jumbling thoughts were taking him, for exhaustion had become a governing factor in causing the twisting mirage of anonymous forms and shapes to tussle for priority inside his head.....sheer and utter exhaustion.... and hunger.... and a wretched, thriving sense of hopelessness.

How long he remained confined within that brief lapse from reality he had no way of telling, but the next thing he was aware of was a voice that was gently spiriting him back from his miserable pit of desperation.

"Sir!......Sir!........Are you alright sir?......Are you ill?"

The words were spoken in such a soft and kindly tone that Charlie was able to ease himself very slowly but stiffly from his hunched over position and into the sweet smiling face of a young woman with sparkling brown eyes beneath the brim of a deep claret coloured bonnet.

"Urm.....Yes...No...No I'm not ill!........thank you miss...," he stammered sheepishly.

"I'm afraid services don't begin for several hours yet," she continued as she pulled her shawl tighter around her shoulders against the morning chill. "That is...if you were meaning to join us inside of course?"

"Well.....no," he replied slightly embarrassed as he glanced round at the building he was seated in front of. "You see.... I'm on the tramp... looking for work.....and I... just stopped here to rest."

But his words seemed to filter away as his eyes shyly absorbed the sincerity in the smile that he was being given from the angel like form before him.

"I was on my way to open the Chapel and to make ready for the service," she explained. "But I can see you've travelled far.....and you must be tired...and hungry?" she stated. "I can offer you toast and dripping and perhaps some mutton chitterlings....if that would help?"

So it was from that moment on that life changed once again for Charles Edward Wilmot, for in Iris Evans he had found the kind of woman that only comes your way once in a lifetime. And over the very welcome breakfast he learned that she had been left as a day old foundling on the doorstep of Daniel Evans the Methodist Minister some fifteen years previous and just three days after he and his wife Myfanwy had arrived in Hockley from their home town of Swansea, to take up his new position. And being in their middle years and childless, the couple had seen it as a sign and had readily taken the child in as their own and named her Iris, it being the favourite flower of the good minister's wife. It was also pointed out to Charlie as he devoured his toast and dripping that the alternative to her being adopted would have meant her being taken into the workhouse and to what horrors that would have meant for an infant.

And despite the fact that her life was somewhat regimented around the demands of the Chapel and the ministry, she did find it rewarding through her contact with the hard working, poverty stricken community that the Chapel served. Quite often she would bring 'waifs and strays' as she referred to them, into the kitchen of the ministers house for something to sustain them through another day and always with her surrogate parents approval. But it seemed that she saw in the young man sitting across the table, someone a little different from the so many that she had sought to help in the past.

"What can you do?" she casually enquired.

"Oh...since I was eight, I've worked with horses in a wheelwright's stables," he replied honestly, not wanting to lie to this true embodiment of an angel of mercy

"I see....that's interesting!" she responded thoughtfully, and without asking for any reasons why he should find himself unemployed and homeless she continued. "Mr Tranter....who is part of the congregation, works as the manager at the Hockley Railway Sidings. Perhaps he might be able to find something for you........would you like me to ask him?"

And so it was that a few days later Charlie found himself in the employ of the Great Western Railway Company as the groom in charge of the three sturdy horses that pulled the various vehicles, which included the cart for the track maintenance crew, a covered parcel wagon and a selection of other smaller carts and drays. It also meant that he was responsible for not only their maintenance and repair but for the stabling and comfort of his three charges, along with their tack and harness and other equipment. It was now in his hands to show that all the experience he had gained in the Thorndyke's stables and by watching and helping in the wheelwrights workshop was not to be wasted and so put to good use.

Apparently, the position had only come vacant a day or so before, when Charlie's predecessor had been caught using the companies cart and pair for his own profitable use. The consequence of this had been his instant sacking.

From the outset it was obvious that the three robust but beautiful creatures took an instant liking to the gentle but firm handling of their new driver, and this did not go unnoticed by Mr Tranter who felt confident enough to even provide a reference to a Mrs Maud Duff, the landlady of a boarding house not a stone's throw from the sidings. This allowed Charlie to be given a room in her house without the usual week in advance, although he was of the opinion that Iris may have had a say in this also, as Mrs Duff turned out to be another member of her Chapel.

So much had happened in such a short time that Charlie found it very hard to accept the good fortune that he seemed to have stepped into quite by accident. To think, that after months of despair, of wandering from place to place, tired, hungry and cold and like so many that he had encountered, accepting that it was very unlikely it would ever change for the better. And then to fall asleep in a goods wagon and to literally climb out of it one early Sunday morning and not even knowing where he was, merely to meet the prettiest young woman he had ever clapped his eyes on and before he knew it he had a position that truly suited him. And to top that, he had comfortable lodgings to boot.

And so it was that over the next weeks and months he not only earned the respect of his fellow workers but that of GWR, the company he worked for and not to mention his three equine workmates Grace, Daisy and Juniper. It was also a period when he got to know Iris better, through their walks along the railway embankment and the quiet moments on the benches in the local park, where they would simply chat and be content in the friendship that was developing between them.

For Iris would talk about the people that the Chapel served, the poor hardworking families barely surviving on the inadequate wages that were brought into the hovels they tried to call home. And about the imbalance between those who had money and were always mercilessly grabbing more and those whose backbreaking and never ending toil was the sum total of their miserable lives. For Charlie this offered an insight into the passionate integrity and spirit that seemed to exude from every pore of this endearing young woman who was capturing his heart. She would expound on so many fervent ideals that she held with such zeal and enthusiasm, ideals that were also beginning to filter through from so many varying quarters of the used and subjugated population of the country and all with the same cry of……

'So many wrongs need to be righted'.

It was over a year after Charlie had first clambered from the goods wagon in Hockley railway sidings and during one of the priceless times of intimate exchanges of one another's hopes and thoughts of a brighter future, that Charlie decided to finally come true with an account of his own tarnished past. Something he had avoided delving into ever since he had first met and spoken with Iris and something that she had never queried or questioned in the hope that one day her Charlie would see fit to trust her.

And so she listened intently to every last syllable that Charlie spoke, absorbing every nuance of the narrative and digesting every miniscule trace of emotion that was in his voice. And when he finished she looked at him for a very long moment before she took his hands in hers.

"My dear," she quietly whispered. "I am not a violent person…… and as a rule I cannot condone it……. However, I am not so sheltered that I am unaware that these things go on…… for every day I hear things that beat at my soul……But this…..this person….. this Peebles was truly evil and needed to be stopped….. Goodness me!…..I cannot even bring myself to utter his given name……a name that has so much meaning for me, because it is a sacred name within the scriptures….. And yet… with your fists you took it upon yourself to undertake the task of stopping this man……And in so doing, I am certain that you prevented not only your auntie from more suffering… but I suspect many….many more besides!"

With that she lifted his hands to her lips and lightly kissed each of his bunched up knuckles in turn, this being the first physical intimacy that had ever been shared between them. And what followed was an unspoken moment of true understanding and unity of spirit between two people.

vi.
No Going Back

And now seated on the wall that fronted the steps of the Methodist Chapel as the moment, that very precious moment flitted lightly into his mind, Charlie lifted his clenched fists up close to his face and he was almost able to sense the gentle touch of her lips brushing against them once again. But as that such endearing sensation was bringing a contented smile to his face another more significant and disturbing factor slipped in to quickly wipe it away. It was the sobering fact that it was three years ago since he had first found the very wall that he was now seated upon.

Three years and so much had changed in his life and for everyone else around him it seemed. For Iris had now taken over as housekeeper of the manse, due to the fact that Mrs Evans was too feeble through her lifetime of servitude to her hard ministering husband. And Mr Evans himself was also beginning to lose the fortitude of purpose that had carried him through his whole life of devoted work.

As for himself, he was still working with his beloved horses and alongside the other passion in his life, the railway and the engines. But true contentment can be marred by intruding thoughts and questions that needed answering and finally putting to rest. For Charlie it had been the gnawing desire to see his home town of Cradley Heath just one more time, so much so that it had became a dominant factor on how he approached each day.

Charlie once again allowed his mind to amble back, but this time a mere twenty four hours. The strange thing was that Iris had known long before he had explained his need to revisit his past just one more time, if only to reassure himself that those he had cared for were not in need of him anymore. And such was the connection that was developing between the two young people that she had not even needed to say a word in reply but had conveyed her understanding by simply placing her soft hand on his cheek and the giving of a knowing smile.

And so with Mr Tranter's permission and by paying one of his workmates out of his own pocket to tend his duties for a day, he had managed to find a ride in the brake van of a goods train heading west in the direction of the Black Country and his home town of Cradley Heath.

Now much broader in the shoulders and sporting a well cultivated bush moustache and looking much more the man he had become, his first call was to his Auntie Nora. But she had married and it pleased Charlie to see a smiling and very different woman than the one he had last seen three years previous. It seemed that it had been a matter of just a few months following his departure that a Mr Horace Fletcher, a widower of two years, briefly courted his auntie and married her, thus bringing the combined families of two adults and seven children under the one roof of the two up two down terraced house in Waterloo Street of Mr Fletcher the tailor.

With his small workshop in the yard at the rear of the house, Horace and Nora and three of the older children worked well together making all kinds of garments from bags of scrap material that Horace obtained or purchased cheap from the workhouse, the local rag and bone man, the hospital, undertakers and numerous other sources. These they washed and then repaired or made into all manner of clothes, including flat caps, shirts, jackets, overcoats and even blankets that they then sold for a profit on their market stall. It seemed that all the hard work that the family put into the venture was at least giving them a reasonable standard of living, which in itself provided good reasons to believe that the next step for them was to extend into opening up a small tailors shop.

His second stop was a very emotional reunion for both Charlie and his beloved sister Agnes. It pleased him to see that she also seemed happy and content with her expanding family which now numbered two girls and two boys. However the sad news was that nothing had been seen or heard of their brother Albert for almost two years. Although to slightly balance this, was the confirmation that both Mr Zephaniah Peebles and Mr William Briggs were now languishing through very long penal sentences in Winson Green Prison.

Finally it was to Thorndyke the Wheelwright and a rather emotive and moving visit to the stables. For the news there was even more upsetting for Charlie, as only a month before Betsy had passed away, leaving Old Joe to become a mere shadow of the man he had once been. And there were tears in the aging groom's eyes as he tried to describe to Charlie the deep sense of loss that he now felt at losing his Betsy, his dear wife of over fifty years and of the pain that the kindly lady had silently endured during the final weeks of her life. Now the only joy the old man seemed to derive was in seeing and knowing that Charlie had come of age and was the man that he had always hoped he would be. And when Charlie related all that had happened to him and the good fortune which had come his way, Old Joe simply placed both his strong hands onto the young man's broad shoulders and looking him straight in the eyes and said.....

"My Betsy would've been so proud of you!"

Charlie straightened his back and raised his head so that his moist eyes could take in the growing morning light above the rooftops of the houses opposite to where he was seated on the wall that fronted the steps of the Methodist Chapel. And as he did so the tired features of Old Joe, the man who had been as good as any father to him slipped again into his mind as he recalled his sad, heart rending departure from Thorndyke's stables just the evening before. For it had been there under the guidance of Old Joe that Charlie had grown from a sapling into a tree, from a boy into a man. And even as they had shared one final firm embrace, each had known in their heart of hearts that it was to be the last time either of them would ever set eyes on the other again.

However, even as Charlie had taken his leave from that so special period of his past, he was confident in the knowledge that Old Joe and the stables were now in the good and trustworthy hands of his young cousin Josh. For it seemed that the lad had taken over, not only the little loft space that Charlie had for many years called home but also a place of respect and affection with Old Joe and equally Mr Thorndyke his employer.

Now with his mind spiralling amongst the memories induced by his brief excursion into his past, some words that Old Joe had spoken to him as he turned to leave buzzed once more around inside his head....

"Time is a cruel dictator," the old man had said with a quiver in his voice, "in that it brings together and then takes away without mercy."

And as he had walked pensively away from Thorndykes there had been only the one point of simple reasoning in his mind and that was born out of the contented knowledge that the past he was leaving behind had no need of him anymore but the future he was walking towards did. And without another glance back he had decided rather coldly, that the past was best left in the past and somewhere never to be revisited again.

With that thought still vividly clear in his mind he dropped his head forward and away from the rooftops opposite to the wall on which he was seated, a place that had become a kind of sanctuary for him over the three years since he had found it, exhausted and lost and very hungry.

Gradually his musings began to take on a more pleasant, reflective nature.

"Three years ago!" he whispered under his breath. "Three years since I first sat on this wall!"

And it was, three years almost to the day that Iris had greeted him on that fateful Sunday morning, when in the early grey light he had, by what twist of fate he had never questioned, somehow stumbled across the wall he was now seated upon, the wall that fronted the steps of the Hockley Methodist Chapel, not knowing where he was, or what the future held for him. And equally, he could not have known just how much life would change for him...... and for Iris.

"Three years.......!" he breathed wistfully.

Just then a voice interrupted his ponderings.

"Good morning Charlie.....I'm so glad to see you've returned safely," Iris sighed with a certain relief in her voice.

Looking up he was greeted by the sweet smile that he had come to know and to love so much, that was even now beaming fondly at him from beneath the white lace fringed, black bonnet that hid the normally long auburn tresses. And to complete the picture of the 'Sunday best' mixed with an air of Wesleyan modesty was the crisp white, frill fronted blouse, full length black skirt and black lace shawl, while the slender fingers clutched a bible and hymn book.

But it was the eyes that Charlie's gaze was momentarily taken in by, for it was within those deep set brown orbs that he was seeing his future as a bright new horizon in a world of transition. From the old of

Queen Victoria, who had so recently passed away to the new that King Edward VII was promising to usher in. Nevertheless, whatever world it was it would be a different world, a world with hope in a better future and a world with his Iris beside him.

And so, the story continues.

****

ODYSSEY OF A QUIET MAN.

Part Two.
THE QUIET MAN.

i.
Platform 7

There is an irresistible magic about a railway station with all the comings and goings of the hustling, bustling surge of people, each with a purpose, each with a reason to be somewhere and each displaying a variety of expressions. From the worried businessman hoping he can make it to his appointment on time, to the woman with a baby in her arms, nervously waiting for her soldier husband who is coming home on leave. Then there is the pious looking vicar and the plump, cheery granny and the furtive young couple, sneaking away to a little B and B in some coastal town or other. And always there are the bored looking porters smoking and lounging on their baggage barrows and the habitual sprinkling of train spotters, whose obsession seems to span all ages.

These and so many, many more with each and every face hiding a story, a secret all their own and never to be shared, only to be guessed at as they flit by in the blink of an eye and then are lost once more into the mingling, blurry throng of anonymous shadowy forms. All the faces of all the varying layers of society that can be observed and scrutinized from the unobtrusive bench outside the Refreshment Rooms on Platform 7 of Snow Hill Station, Birmingham, where Arthur Charles Wilmot would sit quite motionless and quite content, merely to watch and to listen and to drink in from the intoxicating concoction of humanity before him.

And with his senses so finely tuned Arthur would slowly allow his eyelids to drop a little, while he picked out and identified all the other subliminal elements of this wondrous place. From the banging carriage doors and the squeal of luggage trolley wheels, to the guard's shrill whistle and the shuffle of scurrying feet, all blending neatly with the harsh, incoherent platform announcements and the anxious and excited chattering of the waiting passengers. But then there was also that strange, skin tingling buzz, which to Arthur was the inexplicable aura of anticipation that seemed to permeate throughout the whole of the station, from the glass and girder roof high above his head, to everything and everyone below.

All of this was so very familiar to Arthur Wilmot, as were all the other pulsating sounds and evocative smells and aromas that conjure up the uniqueness of a railway station. But to Arthur there was nothing that could even compare with the engines, those hissing, fiery, smoke snorting dragons that Arthur had been so intrigued by, even mesmerized by since he was a boy.

For it was as a boy, waiting on that very bench for his engine driver father to finish his shift that he had discovered the mystical world that had totally absorbed his imagination and curiosity, and which became the fascination that had taken over every waking and dream filled moment of his young life. And even from that early age that gripping obsession had grown each and every time he had walked through the hallowed portal of the booking hall concourse to take his seat outside the Refreshment Rooms on Platform 7.

Although for Arthur in later years, the moments that became most precious to him were when the last timetabled train of the day had chuffed and puffed and clattered out of the station into the darkness beyond and the final weary passengers had found their way to the subway or bridge that led out into the thriving hubbub of the City streets, for it was then the station would seem to breathe a sigh, a deep sigh as if it had been preparing to sleep. And after the sound of the train had finally diminished away into the dark night and the clouds of smoke and steam had begun to clear leaving the hanging platform lights in a misty haze, there was always a silence, a blessed silence that seemed to enfold and hold. And with that silence would come a tranquil peace that descended like a soothing, cool hand across the furrows of Arthur's brow.

Many a time the night staff awaiting the fleeting visit of the mail train, or a cleaner clearing up all the debris of the day would come across Arthur, even in the early hours seated in his usual place on the bench outside the Refreshment Rooms on Platform 7 in quiet, thoughtful meditation. They would simply pass by with nothing more than a curious glance and a little shake of the head, seemingly unwilling to disturb the lonely, insular existence of Arthur Charles Wilmot.

For in Arthur's eyes over the years that bench became a kind of sanctuary, offering a place and a time to reflect and to compose himself from all the day to day trials and tribulations that his whole existence seemed to be confronted by. For Arthur's life had always seen its unfair share of upset and difficulties to contend with and yet those priceless moments in his concept of a cathedral to the permanent way were more like a pilgrimage of faith that brought nothing but comfort to his soul, a comfort that had been devoid elsewhere throughout his lonely and reclusive life.

Even so, to look back on the life of Arthur Charles Wilmot it is important to understand the quiet man and his story. For like all those thousands of brief encounters that he had observed from the bench outside the Refreshment Rooms on Platform 7 of Snow Hill Station Birmingham, Arthur's story is also one that is worthy of a telling.

****

From Arthur's initial entry into the world, it was clear he was going to find life a harsh mix of solitude and self reliance in a society intolerant of something different. Born six weeks premature in 1909 and weighing only one pound one ounce, by every standard of the time he should not have survived. However, his abrupt and rather troubled entry into the world did have its consequences, for whilst Arthur was defying both the attending pharmacist, who came cheaper than a doctor and also the local midwife, the two miscarriages his mother had previously suffered and the boy's difficult delivery left her unable to have more children and for Arthur to grow up weakly and slight of stature, never quite attaining five foot in height.

Almost at the same time as Arthur was winning his first battle the small Wilmot family of Charlie and Iris his parents and Charlotte his older sister by five years, moved a mile or so from the crowded two rooms above an ironmongers shop in Hockley, Birmingham into a rented two up two down terraced house in Digbeth. And with this slight change in the family's fortunes came a sense of hope for the future, with Iris working in the canteen of a local factory making small arms, bicycles and motor cycles and Charlie, an engine driver out of Snow Hill Station.

However, from the outset the first few years were not easy ones for the young Arthur. Because of his frail, undersized physique he would try to avoid contact with everyone outside his family circle, resulting in him being a rather shy, withdrawn child who found his only true form of comfort and reassurance was by the protective side of Charlotte his older sister.

It seemed inevitable therefore that much came to be expected of Charlotte, but it was a mantel that she wore willingly and in full knowledge that she was the one person who Arthur seemed to have complete trust in with all things. So it was, even from the early days of Arthur's infancy, that she tended to shoulder all the constant demands of a boy who stood out as being frail and seriously self conscious, in an inherent class structure that was always going to favour the strongest and the fittest. Furthermore, it was she who somehow became the confidante of all the odd little quirks of growing up that Arthur suffered from and he appeared to have so many more than the street hardened youngsters of the working class area that the family lived in. And although Charlotte found this all to be very challenging, it did encourage a deep bond to develop between herself and her younger brother, a bond that Arthur came to rely on more and more as time went by.

But there was one other overriding ingredient in his upbringing besides the closeness that grew and he thrived on with his older sister, it was the firm stability that he gained from being a part of a loving, caring family. A family provided for by parents working hard for their children in those difficult and arduous times of living in the wake of the Edwardian era.

So Arthur Wilmot continued to struggle with growing up and preparing for the big wide world of school, although his total lack of confidence and self esteem, along with the diminutive nature of his physique threatened to severely hamper any progress his parents might have been hoping for. And this sense of pessimism was heightened the moment that Arthur stepped through the school gates on his first morning at the age of five, merely to stand frozen to the spot with a tight, tearless expression etched deep into his small facial features as he was subjected to the taunts and ridicule from the other taller and older children who stood pointing and gesticulating in Arthurs direction. Even within the first few weeks it was glaringly obvious that apart from the hostility which was constantly being aimed at Arthur, the whole school process appeared to be a very unfavourable and daunting environment for the shy, inoffensive elfin like Arthur Wilmot. A school process that even at the beginning of the twentieth century was designed to cope with the whole rather than the individual, with class sizes disproportionate with the availability of competent teachers and which could only lead to Arthur receiving a very disjointed and punishing education to say the least.

However, the cold dispassionate mask that Arthur was increasingly capable of portraying really disguised a brightness of intellect that could have remained buried and lost behind the confines of his defensive wall. Fortunately though his astute and perceptive older sister saw beyond the barrier and took it upon herself to place her younger brother under her wing and simply teach him everything that she was being taught herself. And over time she found that the newly unearthed sharpness of Arthurs mind made him a very receptive and intuitive pupil indeed.

So with the little in the three R's that he could glean from the classroom, his sister would augment with her evening sessions of private tuition, while his mother Iris would guide him along his moral pathway through her Sunday School classes at the local Methodist Chapel. And so for Arthur and the Wilmot family, there was at least a certain fulfilling simplicity about the way that the family life was beginning to turn out.

And yet, no one can say what lies ahead, for no one can predict the future even though the signs seem always to have been there. For human nature has the ability to bury its head in the sand and hope the truth will go away. As it was for the Wilmot family and so many millions of other families throughout the country, throughout the whole civilized world for that matter who were content to muddle through with their lives in their own way. But when the evil threat of war finally becomes a devastating reality, out of necessity the life that man had must then be put on hold.

So it was that on the 28th July 1914 the world changed forever and not least for the Wilmot family, with Charlie volunteering and joining the merry throng of young men who marched off to their destinies with such a joyous sense of adventure. Then over the next four years those who returned were either broken through their wounds or mere tortured shells of the men they were before, although sadly so many never did return.

However, the cynics and anti war mongers had great satisfaction pointing out that, of all those who had marched away to war just who were the lucky ones. Was it those who returned embittered and morose with either their bodies or their minds destroyed forever or was it those that had been left behind, rotting in no man's land or lost in some mass grave or other to merely become a memory to those who had waved them off to war. For at least then they would be remembered for who they had been, and not seen and pitied for what they had become.

It was in the autumn of 1916 that Charlie came home deeply traumatised and a victim of a mustard gas attack. Apart from the deep mental anguish resulting from what he had seen and experienced in the trenches, the gas had left him badly scarred from the blister burns on his hands, arms, legs, face and neck. It also caused burns to his lungs which were to leave him with asthma and serious respiratory problems for the rest of his life.

But it was seeing the shadow of the man that had been his father walk through the door of their house and break down, sobbing like a child into the arms of his wife which seriously affected Arthur. Even so Charlie stubbornly refused to talk about his experiences in the trenches, never allowing his family to even have a glimpse of the horrors that this decent, honest man had witnessed. Although, anyone with any imagination could not fail to see it all in the dark heavy lines on his face and the constant, deep rooted hurt in his eyes.

That said, the saddest part for the young Arthur was to see his father sitting in his favourite fireside chair, lost in his thoughts while sucking on his empty pipe, for since his return it had remained unlit for fear of it causing him to erupt into another disturbing spasm of rasping, phlegmy coughing. And yet, it was the night times and lying awake in his bed that Arthur loathed the most, for it was then that he would again see the troubled hurt in his father's eyes and truly wish that in some way he was able to absorb all the soulful grief that it was causing the man that he loved and admired.

But to the world at large this was never made apparent, simply because by the time Arthur had reached the age of seven years old he had learnt never to exhibit any signs of weakness or emotion. And over the subsequent years he continued to nurture the morbid ability to fervently guard against any show of sensitivity or empathy and as a consequence he gained a reputation for being remote and impassive, something of a rather 'cold fish' even to those closest to him.

Nevertheless, some good did come out of his father's return, for the severity of his wounds meant he avoided being sent back to the trenches and because he had been so well thought of at Snow Hill Station he was able to go back to a job with the railway. Sadly though this was not to be as a driver of his beloved engines, for it was felt that the heat and smoke on the footplate would only aggravate his condition and so he was offered a place in the maintenance sheds.

But to Charlie it was a job and a job in the one work place that he wanted to be in. And if he had needed a tonic to help lift him out of the cruelly depressed doldrums he had been wallowing in since coming home from the hell of the western front, then it was that little bit of good fortune. It also meant that Arthur was able to reunite himself with the bench outside the Refreshment Rooms on Platform 7, the little piece of heaven that he had been forced to forfeit during his father's two year absence.

So for a while at least life became as near to normal as the war years would allow, with Iris continuing to work in the canteen at the local factory, which had now turned to making armaments and Charlie back in the world he knew and understood, simply by helping to keep the trains running.

Then as the war ended in November 1918, the Wilmot family like the rest of the country attempted to settle back into rebuilding their lives while desperately trying to put the previous four years of horror as far behind them as their tainted memories would allow.

But for Arthur this merely meant the torturous continuation of his school years, for the small, weakly child still suffered badly at the hands of the bullies. Daily he would run the gauntlet and the spiteful taunts of his stronger, taller peers, but over the years he managed to develop the tenacity to ride over their abuse. Although, at least one teacher did become aware of the diminutive pupil's troubles and tended to provide him with some small task to keep him away from the hands of his tormentors.

All this did have a detrimental effect on Arthur, for unhappily he became known as the teacher's favourite which only added to the unwanted attention he habitually received. Even so, Arthur's ice cold disposition prevented him from ever displaying how deep the cut of humiliation was that their actions were really causing him, which only went to frustrate his abusers even more. The outcome of this was that he progressed through his formative years without one single individual of his own age that he could call a friend.

So once again it fell upon the willingness of Charlotte, to this time take on the role of friend and to combine it with her already established tasks of mentor and guide. Although, it could be said, that this arrangement now had the effect of totally denying her brother of his childhood and the experience of growing up amongst his contemporaries, something that is integral to the developing adolescent. On the other hand it did seem to provide Arthur with a very welcome cushion from an outside world that had more than proven itself to be increasingly alien and hostile the older he had become and as a consequence it was far more demanding and difficult to cope with. Either way could be viewed to be both right and wrong for their own varying reasons, but each could also be viewed as damaging and detrimental to Arthur's growth and progress and to leave the question of what would be the long term ramifications on Arthur.

And it is a fact that what cannot be seen on the surface does not actually mean that deep down no hurt or lasting harm was being inflicted, but Arthur had become so adept at masking his emotions that even his family were ever fully aware of what lay beneath the cold, impenetrable exterior of its youngest member.

In truth, although Charlie and Iris worked tirelessly to provide a good home for their children, it was Charlotte who manoeuvred Arthur through those difficult years towards his adolescence. And as a result of the devotion and affection she selflessly bestowed on him, the boy developed such a deep love and belief in his sister that was to last all the days of his life, even after Charlotte's untimely death through tuberculosis in 1922 at the age of eighteen.

However, it was Charlotte's long painful passing that bequeathed on her younger brother a deep, deep scar on his heart and a gaping, fathomless crevasse of emptiness in his life that was never to be filled. And in coping with the devastating significance of her death, Arthur's mind and senses became so numbed that he was able to slam the door shut on any possibility of an outpouring of grief or sentiment of any kind. So much so that all anyone saw was an undersized, adolescent boy whose countenance and the whole of his body for that matter displayed nothing but a complete void of any form of emotion whatsoever.

Even as Arthur stood by the death bed of his beloved sister, he was not even capable of shedding one single tear. He merely stared down at the pale, yet pretty lines of her finely sculptured cheek bones and cupids bow lips that had always been able to turn heads in admiration. And it was as his eyes soaked up in grim fascination his beloved sister's peaceful features, he was able to shield himself behind his defence lines that forbade him to even provide the faintest glimmer into that secret sanctuary of his soul. And it can only be imagined what actual pit of hurt and despair he was actually experiencing, for there was nothing, nothing to identify that he was feeling anything at all.

Standing there statue like and silent within his own rhythmic breathing, he remained immobile and unflinching, rejecting any submission to a show of emotion that was so opposed to his cold, expressionless facade that in fact denied the intensity of the moment of closeness and spiritual affinity that he was inwardly sharing with his sister.

There was however, one momentary instance of a real and moving show of feeling from Arthur and it came with the sudden realisation that his precious sister was now free of the all consuming pain that she had suffered throughout her illness, for in her brother's eyes Charlotte thankfully appeared to be finally at peace. But that moment of weakness on the part of her brother was soon short lived, before the frozen veil of indifferent isolation was once more drawn back into place.

Many hours went by with Arthur standing in lonely vigil, absorbing every detail of his sister's features in the flickering yellowy glow of a solitary candle. And it was as the candle began to splutter itself out that Arthur finally stretched forward to gently stroke his sister's long auburn hair that could glint with golden strands in the sunlight. The gentle stroking of those long silky tresses was an action that he had undertaken almost every evening since he had been old enough to stand behind his sister and hold her hairbrush. The mere act of the brushing and the stroking of her hair as she had softly and slowly counted from one to one hundred to correspond with each gentle downward motion of the brush had come to be regarded by Arthur as simply nothing less than a true labour of love.

And with those luscious curls held loosely in his fingers once more, he was able to relive that sense of oneness, of being in tune that had been afforded to them both merely through the action of the brushing of the hair at bedtime. An action that was something so simple and yet so profound, that even as Arthur swooned over that unity of spirit that he had prized so much, he was again able to envisage so clearly in his mind's eye his sister sitting and smiling at him through her reflection in the dressing table mirror, while he lovingly brushed that long, soft, delicate auburn mane. And it was that very rare but warm sense of shared deep affection and empathy, that even in death the touch of her hair was once again able to rekindle in Arthur.

It was then with one final, deliberate act that he took from his trouser pocket his mother's darning scissors and tenderly cut a two inch long curl from the end of his sister's flowing hair. This he then secreted away in a small leather envelope, which in turn was hidden from sight for only his eyes to ever to see again. An innocent act of remembrance you might say, to take that snippet of his sister's hair, but to Arthur it was something so heartfelt and necessary, so vitally important to him that he was to keep it with him as his one and only truly abiding comfort throughout his life. To Arthur it was a symbol, a simple embodiment of the love and belief that he bore for his sister.

So it was that Arthur walked away from that sad scene, carefully concealing the small leather envelope containing his sister's precious wisp of hair, along with the seething pain of losing his one and only true and sincere friend so early in their lives.

But sadly more hurt was to follow just twelve months later in 1923, when Iris his mother also succumbed to the deadly tuberculosis. But Arthur in that moment of even more deep sorrow was again seen to be devoid of any outward display of feelings or emotion, being completely lacking of any show of sorrow or sentiment, or to even be able to dignify his mothers passing with the shedding of at least one tear. He was not even capable of consoling his distraught father, who would sit in his favourite chair by the fire and weep uncontrollably like a child. Enough it seemed to Arthur, for the two of them.

Nevertheless, it was a few days after his mother's funeral that Arthur once again found himself on the bench outside the Refreshment Rooms on Platform 7 of Snow Hill Station while waiting for his father's shift to finish, but now with much to occupy his mind. For his head seemed to reel with morose, oppressive thoughts which reflected the inner tussle that he was feeling about his past and his future and all of which only went to emphasise his utter isolation and sense of loss even more. And yet the true impact of the sadness of those thoughts never even contaminated the ingrained bland expression on his face. Although, he did find that he needed to take in several deep breaths in an attempt to shake off a sudden, strange quivering that seemed to run freely, like chilly fingers up and down his spine.

A strange stirring that in point of fact was merely adolescent emotion striving to surface and upset the normally well controlled equilibrium. But it concerned Arthur for a moment and the maturing man inside the boy considered its significance to be a warning of never to allow his guard to drop again. And so, with a deep shudder and a sigh, Arthur's single minded sense of purpose came back to shield him, to screen him from prying eyes and without any change to his blank, impassive demeanour he continued to gaze pensively at all the mingling, meandering figures going about their business along his beloved Platform 7.

Sitting there on his bench, the brief emotional spark now quenched, Arthur's thoughts began to move along more philosophical pathways, for being at the age of fourteen Arthur also had to come to terms with the fact that he would never reach five foot tall or exceed seven stone in weight. However, he had learnt to accept this in a fatalistic manner, absorbing any sly looks or snide innuendo's that where aimed in his direction by walking away in a quiet and dignified manner.

This all added to the persona that in some ways was contrived for self preservation and in other ways being deeply instilled in him from years of the unwanted attention his diminutive stature would attract. For it was at those upsetting times that Charlotte had always been there to protect him from such situations and he missed her. He missed her for the fact of knowing that she had been totally and without any reservations on his side.

However, since that fateful day of Charlotte's death he had made his way on a Sunday morning to the cemetery at Hockley to stand by her grave. There he would speak in silent words about his most deep felt inner feelings. And it was there looking down on the final resting place of his beloved sibling that he was also able to hear her soft voice speaking to him with words of perfect wisdom, words that helped to guide him through the trials of everyday life. Even in death she was still his soul mate, his confidante.

"Charlotte!" he would whisper.

Then staring wistfully at her silent grave he would once again try to visualise her, there in front of him with her smile so tender and inviting and so easily illustrating the warmth that had always been in her heart. He would try to imagine her long auburn hair that could glint with golden strands in the sunlight, when disturbed by some wayward breeze.

"Charlotte," he would silently murmur to himself. "Oh.... Charlotte!"

And with her name still humming loud in his mind he would seek out the one thing that could give him the comfort that his troubled soul demanded, by reaching into his jacket pocket and drawing out the small leather envelope that contained the precious cutting of his sister's auburn hair. With great care he would slip his fore finger into the envelope to lightly touch the soft strands within and as he did so a rush of scintillating warmth would course through the whole of his body. It was a sensation that occurred each time that he touched those fine strands and each time his senses would thrill to it without him really understanding why. And yet, almost as quickly as he felt those precious auburn strands against his finger tip, all feelings of anxiety and concern would subside and leave him once more with a strange, eerie sense of euphoria that would confuse the innocent nature of the boy even more.

But now it was the heavy rumbling and trundling and snorting of an engine approaching Platform 7 that finally made young Arthur lift himself from his ponderous musings and slowly and with great care he replaced the small leather envelope once more to the safety of his jacket pocket. For even though his mind for the moment had been by his sisters grave side, the leather envelope had somehow appeared in his fingers without him really knowing how it had got there.

And this quiet, intensely reserved boy, who even now was teetering on the brink of manhood, surveyed his favourite view for the thousandth time and gave a deep penetrating sigh of contentment. Even so, on this occasion it was a sigh that was slightly flawed by a certain throbbing mix of anguish and uncertainty for the future and a sense of overwhelming sorrow for the present and the past. Yet in spite of that, none of the daunting thoughts for one so young could be detected in any part of his facial expression or bearing.

Sitting there, drinking in the view along Platform 7 from the bench outside the Refreshment Rooms of Snow Hill Station, he was able to abstract his thinking away from all that was disturbing him and concentrate on what he was seeing as something so perfect that in his eyes could never be tainted in any way.

ii.
Alone

Almost a year later, in 1924 Charlie's health finally submitted to the effects of the gas attack he had suffered in the trenches of 1916 and it was then that the fifteen year old Arthur came to realise exactly what loneliness really meant.

Standing over his father's grave as the half dozen or so of his father's railway work mates slowly dispersed, an overwhelming sense of sheer isolation and solitude engulfed Arthur and this time there was no reassuring hand on his shoulder to lessen the feeling of grief that he could feel but could never show. And even as the weight of the moment bore down on him he was still not able to shed one single tear, not one single tear in tribute to the last remaining member of his family. There was not even the merest change in the cold stare in his eyes, or the slightest flinch in his tight jawed, expressionless features. However, all this merely concealed the fact that deep down inside Arthur there was such a throbbing sadness that burned and smouldered like the fire in the fire box of the railway engines that he loved to watch.

And yet, even at his young age, Arthur was aware that the beating sadness was not merely for the passing of the one constant point in his life, it was also for himself. For merging within the heat of that sadness were the glowing embers of despair, not only for the moment and what to do next but also the despair of what that next move would lead to. He was alone now, alone in a world that was foreign to him, a world that he did not understand and in which he was like a person treading water in the hope that someone just might throw him a lifeline.

Since infancy he had always found protection with his sister Charlotte, who had even fought his battles for him in the school playground. And then there had been his mother with her soft words of comfort and his father who had guided him away from the harshness of his existence which had now inadvertently left him unprepared for a future without those firm influences to show him the way.

But as he stood alone in the cemetery in the drizzling rain, looking down at his father's simple wooden cross a sudden resolve entered his frail frame like a bolt of lightning that caused a shudder to run right through him. The realisation was saying to him in a loud, clear voice that he must be a man and not the child that his family had always tried to protect from the outside world, that he now knew he must face on his own. But there was no one to show him direction, to point him forward and as a consequence he was viewing the future as merely being able to survive the day and then to worry about tomorrow when it arrived.

And that is where the confusion lay for Arthur, for in truth he had the brightness of intellect to know that he was just treading water and waiting for that elusive lifeline to be thrown, but he was equally mindful that in reality his salvation must be by his own hand and therefore he must now learn to swim.

Later that afternoon and standing in the street outside the house with the rented two rooms he had shared with his father since his mother died, he wondered again where the next step into his future would lead him. For the reality was that now he had nothing, the two rooms had gone because the rent had not been forthcoming, in the same way as the house in Digbeth had gone following his mother's death. And what possessions that had been in the rooms had all been sold to help pay for his father's funeral, the funeral that his railway work mates had come together to organise because Arthur had been incapable of even that duty.

Even so, apart from his father's scarf and the clothes he stood up in Arthur had managed to secrete away a small collection of his own prized possessions. There was the Hornby clockwork railway set and the small wooden engine that his father had carefully carved for Arthur's eighth birthday while recovering from his wounds. And then there were the meticulously collected cigarette cards of railway engines and the well read Boys Own annuals. All of which Arthur had carried away in the large leather engine driver's tool bag that his father had used for his sandwiches, his enamel tea can and oil skin and all the other things he needed to take to his work. The large leather bag that was more like a small suitcase against the boy's diminutive frame and which now held all those items of extreme personal value to the boy in Arthur, but which were totally useless to the man that he must now become.

But this simply epitomised the glowing guileless nature of Arthur. For in collecting and making sure of his own special belongings he had neglected to pick up any of the essentials for survival, such as what food there might still have been in the rooms, or even his heavy coat for warmth.

And as darkness fell and the chill began to bite through the cardigan his mother had knitted for him, desperation also took hold of his meagre frame to the point that he not only shivered with the cold but with the daunting thought of what to do next. With his eyes staring wistfully, almost hopefully up at the window of the rooms he had so recently vacated when the coffin of his father had been carried out that morning, the demoralizing isolation of his situation took an even firmer hold on him. For the boy in Arthur was still trying to will that elusive lifeline to be thrown down to him, even though the slowly emerging man deep within him was now telling him that it was not going to happen.

But still he was unable to draw himself away from all that he had known, simply because he had nowhere else to focus on, nowhere else to go. It was as if the life that he had known had been buried with his father and that what lay before him was a blank, fathomless abyss in his mind, and it was significant that even the small leather envelope that contained his sister's lock of auburn hair seemed to deny him the solace that his soul was now yearning for.

However, there is always the possibility of a Good Samaritan in any community and it was Mr and Mrs Lambert from the shop at the end of the street, who had watched the solitary figure all through the afternoon and who were the ones to finally come to Arthur's rescue. For the boy's father had become friendly with the old couple by patronising their shop for groceries and newspapers. It had been during one of the early loose exchanges across the counter that it had come to light that Charlie had known the couples only son, who had been killed at the Battle of Ypres in April 1915. The resulting conversations between Arthur's father and the Lamberts then helped to develop a friendship which the old couple came to respect by offering Charlie's fledgling son a place of safety and a place to finalise his maturing years.

At the back of the shop was a small room which the Lamberts offered to the timid, bewildered boy along with his meals and a small wage and in return he would become their errand boy cum assistant in the shop. This was a decision that they had reached, more out of pity than for any rational reason, simply after watching the wretched image that the forlorn and lost young Arthur had portrayed throughout the afternoon. An image that had brought tears of maternal sadness to the sympathetic eyes of Mrs Lambert, and tears that her husband always found irresistible in his wife and which always left him incapable of refusing her anything.

And as Arthur sat on his bed on that first night in the meagre glow of a candle, his cold, remote bearing extinguishing any possible lapse towards an emotional reaction at facing manhood and the big wide world alone, there were no tears in his eyes. In fact there was nothing that could be misconstrued as even a child's immature reaction to the distressing events of the day, for there was nothing, merely a sightless, resolute stare into oblivion.

Even sleep failed to entrap the sad young boy that first night, instead he lay wide eyed and motionless until the guttering candle finally flickered out and the pale dawn gradually began to illuminate the sky beyond the small window to his room. In fact, when Mrs Lambert came to take him to the flat above the shop for his breakfast he was still dressed and seated on the bed in the same position as when she had left him the night before. And as he followed her through the shop and up the stairs into the compact little kitchen, it is impossible to even try to imagine what must have been spiralling through the thriving naivety of his mind and what he believed the future might hold for him.

Nevertheless, as the days began to stretch out into weeks, an undiscovered side to Arthur, that even he had been unaware of, began to filter through. This was something akin to a previously untapped reservoir of self reliance and willpower that now, out of necessity appeared to come to the fore to guide him on how he approached his days in the strange, bewildering surroundings that he found himself in. Whatever it was it helped to give a fresh meaning and purpose to Arthur that looked beyond the sturdy walls of his sheltered upbringing within his caring and loving family fortress, to where life meant standing on his own two feet and accepting that there was no easy path for him to tread anymore.

Although for Arthur with his small wiry frame, this was sometimes very difficult to accept, especially when struggling with the heavy lifting of boxes and stock and there was the contact with the various customers to contend with also, which certainly added enormous pressure on his innately reticent and withdrawn nature. But if anything it was the confusing and numbing array of the items that were displayed on the shelves and in the stockroom that caused his head to buzz and flutter when Mr Lambert asked him to either fetch this or to carry that.

And there was one, even more formidable challenge for Arthur when he was required to master the shop delivery bicycle, even though he had never ridden a bicycle before. But the new found single mindedness in him managed to overcame this daunting and potentially hazardous task by the simple strategy of the levelling of the seat down to the crossbar and then by sheer, plucky persistence and numerous scrapes to his knees.

But even though all this tended to overwhelm Arthur's clouded outlook on life, not once did he allow any of his doubts or misfortunes to alter his stony, expressionless reserve, or to be made apparent to the Lamberts. So much so that even after a somewhat apprehensive beginning, when the good couple had wondered at the full extent of the responsibility they had taken on, they came to find that they had very little to complain about from their so willing and honest assistant, who seemed to compensate in some small way for the dear son that they had lost at the tender age of twenty one.

Equally, there was a real sense of underlying pride for them when many of those who came into contact with Arthur had nothing but good words to say about him and would express them openly, even in Arthur's hearing. And the boy, over time seemed to accept his fate philosophically by applying himself to the hard, demanding work and long hours at the Lambert's small shop with a firm but quiet resolve and determination.

In spite of all this, at the end of each day Arthur came to find the bed and the seclusion that his small room offered a very welcoming place to be. It was there that he could shut out all the pressing demands of the day and immerse himself in the consoling comfort of the contents of his father's large leather tool bag. The leather tool bag that contained the Hornby clockwork railway set, the carved engine, the cigarette cards of railway engines and the Boys Own Annuals. But most importantly there was the small leather envelope containing the lock of his sister Charlotte's long auburn hair that could glint with golden strands in the sunlight. All of this and the memories they evoked, being so very precious to him.

Even so there was one small light in a very long week for Arthur, and that was Thursday afternoons. Due to the fact that this was half day closing for the shop it now came to be of immense importance to the young Arthur, for come rain or shine he would first visit the cemetery at Hockley to spend a few moments at each of the graves of his mother and father and then to something of a timeless vigil of silent conversation with his sister Charlotte at her graveside. It was there that he could unburden his troubled soul in complete confidence that no one but his sister would be listening and therefore all those thoughts and fears that crowded his head in the lonely hours of the night time in his little room, could in some way be laid to rest. And each time it was in company with the small leather envelope containing the so precious strands of his sisters auburn hair.

And over the ensuing years those short periods of cherished conversing with his beloved sibling were to become more and more important to him.

From there he would catch the tram back into Birmingham and then run the short distance to Snow Hill Station and the bench outside the Refreshment Rooms on Platform 7. There, with the sandwich and slice of cake that Mrs Lambert provided for his lunch he would sit and savour all the myriad sounds and sights of this, his idea of the most perfect place on earth.

The hours would then pass slowly in sublime reflection for Arthur as he watched and observed all the nameless forms that made up the melting pot of humanity that was the platform of a busy railway station. Watching and observing as they jostled and weaved in anticipation of the next train's arrival or departure and all without exception, having a purpose and a reason for being there and this included Arthur, even though he considered himself to be nothing more than a mere sideline observer. The fact was that he had long been accepted as an integral part of the whole picture by many of the staff, from the chatty porters to the engine drivers and firemen and guards who would call or wave in passing, for many had been work mates of Arthur's father and had known him since his infant days waiting on that very bench.

Even the kindly ladies in the Refreshment Rooms had taken a somewhat motherly shine to the pleasant, diminutive young man and when the seat on which he sat got decidedly chilly they would often bring him a steaming hot cup of cocoa. But even without the cocoa, nothing ever deterred Arthur from this place of sanctuary in an otherwise lonely existence. And even after three years in the employ of the Lamberts he never ever missed a single Thursday afternoon.

For all that, things rarely remain the same for very long and it was in Arthur's eighteenth year that change, out of necessity happened. It was when the good Mr Lambert passed away after a short illness and Mrs Lambert decided to sell the shop.

With much regret but with grateful thanks to Mrs Lambert, who in the short time since her husband's death had gone to look so tired and frail beyond her years, Arthur took his leave to become the office boy in the dispatch and accounts department of Mr Edward Chadwick's Premier Bakeries. This was a position that had been secured for Arthur by Mrs Lambert, through the friendship of her late husband with Mr Chadwick.

But the Arthur Charles Wilmot, who was to become such an indispensible member of Mr Chadwick's staff, was now a young man, still slight of stature but stronger and much more confident than the boy who had stood with his precious belongings packed into the large leather tool bag, outside the rooms he had shared with his father only three years before. And a positive consequence of his new position was that he was now totally independent, with a small but living wage that allowed him a room in Mrs Hinchcliffe's boarding house, just off the Hagley Road in Birmingham. It also meant that his weekly excursions to the cemetery and then to the bench outside the Refreshment Rooms on Platform 7 were now changed to Sundays.

So it was that this very private, reserved young man was at last able to face the world head on, for something had matured within him over his time at the Lamberts shop which was allowing him to view the future with a much more positive and open frame of mind. And by diligent hard work at Chadwick's Premier Bakeries he progressed within four years to Delivery Clerk and then five years later to the elevated and respected position of Senior Purchasing and Accounts Controller.

Having said that, the strange anomaly of Arthur's employment at Chadwick's was that Mr Chadwick and indeed all the other members of his family and even the employees at the Bakeries could honestly admit, that not one of them was ready to say that they actually knew the quiet and enigmatic Arthur Wilmot. But the one thing that they did know was that over the years he had proven himself to be such a valued addition to the firm, winning the respect and trust of everyone that he had dealings with through his honest and straightforward manner. Even so, such was the staunch, introverted nature of the man that he allowed no one to pierce the strong veneer of his self imposed sense of isolation.

Life for Arthur Wilmot now seemed to have a certain perfection and routine to it which suited the simplicity that his solitary, uncomplicated nature so craved. And apart from the notable increase in his wages that his new responsible position carried, there was the added little benefit of the whole of the weekend away from his desk.

However, it was on one particular Sunday morning early in September 1939, that Arthur's little world was to change once more. It was when Mr Chamberlain the Prime Minister formally announced to the country that Britain was again at war with Germany.

Arthur heard the announcement being made along with a stunned gathering of railway staff and passengers around the wireless set in the kitchen of the Refreshment Rooms on Platform 7. And as the little throng silently listened and absorbed what was being said, it has to be considered what thoughts passed through their minds. For not a single soul there could fail to wonder at what cost those damning words would have on each one of them until it was all finally over.

Whilst preparations for war had been underway for some years before that fateful day, what hostilities there were in the first few months were thankfully kept away from home shores, so life in Britain hardly altered. And although Arthur avidly followed the developments of what was commonly referred to as the phoney war through the newspapers and wireless news, it all seemed to be a million miles from his door and of no real concern to him. Even when he thought back on the day he had sat on his special bench and watched hundreds of children being evacuated by train, there in front of him on Platform 7 of Snow Hill Station and just days after war had been declared, he had not appreciated the real impact of the situation even then.

However, the somewhat unnerving standoff situation with Germany could not last and it was in the late spring of 1940 that everything changed with first Norway and then one by one in quick succession Denmark, Holland, Belgium, Luxemburg and then France falling and all in a matter of a few weeks. And even though war was now on Britain's doorstep it was still the other side of the English

Channel and it was commonly considered that the great defensive moat that had kept all invaders at bay since William the Conqueror would again come to the country's aid.

But those that sleep inevitably must wake and Arthur was brought to full wakeful awareness on the first Sunday in June 1940 while watching from the security of the bench outside the Refreshment Rooms on Platform 7. It was then that the war and its consequences were brought brutally into devastating perspective for this shy, retiring individual.

All that day he sat watching in a dawning reality as train after train pulled into the station with all the returning soldiers who had survived the onslaught of the sudden German Blitz Krieg through Belgium and France and had managed to reach the beaches of Dunkirk. And there were even more trains bringing home the wounded who were either assisted or stretchered away by an army of doctors, nurses, ARP wardens and numerous volunteers, with tea and sandwiches and cigarettes being provided by the ladies of the WRVS.

And yet, the most daunting aspect for Arthur were the drawn, desolate features of a defeated army disembarking before him from the crowded carriages, their faces full of the horrors of what they had endured and lived through etched deep into their gaunt expressions. And within each grey and distraught countenance that passed by, Arthur instantly reflected on his own father's grim appearance on his return from the trenches in 1916.

It was as Arthur watched that wretched and seemingly endless procession that something stirred inside him that he had never known or even considered before. For the first time in his life he saw himself as only half a man. Yet it was not a self criticism of the limitations of his own stature, it was something far more profound in him that was saying he was not like all those heroes, all those broken and wounded men who had simply been doing their duty for their king and country. Arthur was getting a very forceful and intense insight that was far beyond his own experience and it was having a very sobering and acute effect on him.

Here he was at the age of thirty one, taking a long searching look at himself and even though he was quietly content with his good, respected position in a family firm, it now seemed that it was not enough, for he wanted more. He wanted to be able to prove to himself that there was more to him than just sitting safely behind a desk, merely making sure that those areas under his jurisdiction were efficient and beyond reproach, even with all the belt tightening caused through the restrictions and rationing that the war was imposing on Chadwicks and everyone else.

No! the stirrings he was feeling were the stirrings of his conscience being activated and it was demanding he did something defining, something that in later years he could sit on the bench outside the Refreshment Rooms on Platform 7 and reflect on with a sense of pride. And so, after almost a fortnight of much thought and deliberation, he dutifully presented himself at the Army Recruitment office only to be disappointed when he was categorized as grade D 'Unfit for any form of military service'.

But this setback did not deter Arthur, for all his adult life he had learnt that the only way forward for him was always the hard way and if he could not be fit and trusted enough to be given a rifle to fight with, he would find another way of achieving his aims. And so after a great deal of persistence on his part he finally found his niche and this was to be as a medical orderly with the Royal Army Medical Corp.

Within a matter of weeks of being accepted, Arthur Wilmot stepped into the second world war with both feet and it was then that the concealed intellect that his sister Charlotte had identified and had brought to the fore all those years ago was now able to shine for itself. It seemed that Arthur had the capability to adapt himself to all the many varied intricacies of his duties in an intelligent and forthright manner. And his cold, unshakable approach now came across as being keen and well adjusted for all the work that he was to be confronted by, especially when he was posted to active fields of conflict.

It was an ironic fact that even with his small stature he was now able to gain the self esteem that his soul had been deprived of. This was achieved by the lasting respect and high opinion that was shown by all those he worked with, from his commanding officer right down to the doctors, nurses and ambulance drivers and all those he came into contact with, including the patients he attended. His innate coldness of nature and sense of emotional indifference combining with his single minded attitude in all things, earned him nick names such as 'Frosty' and 'The Iceman'.

In some ways the names pleased Arthur, for it gave him a strange kind of identity and individualism that he had never enjoyed before. For unlike the abusive names that he had been subjected to as a youngster these nick names were never used in a demeaning manner but in something more of a respectful way of recognising the quiet, professionalism this quiet, solitary yet likable man showed in every aspect of his work.

And yet, it must also be remembered that although Arthur had been classified as grade D 'Unfit for any form of military service' he saw honourable service in North Africa, Crete, Italy and Malta. In each theatre of conflict that Arthur served in he was never far from the actual fighting, many times acting as a field medical orderly under enemy fire. Indeed he developed such a determined and fervent sense of purpose to his work that he was always able to detach himself completely from all the gruesome sights and sounds and even thoughts of personal danger.

In many ways it was as if he had been waiting all of his reclusive and insular life for the opportunity to stand up and be counted as an equal to the rest of the male gender. And his role within the ranks of the RAMC offered him that chance to start from a level platform as every other member of the forces who were fighting for their country's very existence.

On D Day the 6th June 1944, he even landed with the second wave of British troops on Sword beach, attending to both allied and enemy wounded alike without distinction. From there he continued to follow on closely with the allied advance through France and Belgium and into Germany itself, where on one day in late May 1945 he was able to stand before the very bunker in Berlin where Hitler's final days had been spent before his suicide that brought an end to the war and his reign of terror.

So it was that Medical Orderly Corporal Arthur Charles Wilmot came home and thankfully unscathed to civilian life in 1946 but with a slightly proud lift in his step and a much wider view of mankind and the world alike. And although so much had changed whilst he had been away and not least in himself, he viewed the part of his life that he was leaving behind to be best left in the past. It was a characteristic of the man to be able to discern what the important factors in his life were worth consideration and to disregard those that were not. Therefore, he adamantly resigned himself to keep all that had gone before, along with all the abiding memories and experiences secreted and locked away in the far recesses of his mind, never to be referred to again.

iii.
Oakshott Road

It was inevitable, that on his return the first place Arthur would visit was the bench outside the Refreshment Rooms on Platform 7 of the rather bomb battered Snow Hill Station. With something of a 'finally coming home' feeling surging through him, he gratefully took his seat on the bench and began to breathe in deeply from all the easily remembered smells and aromas that he drew in willingly through flared nostrils. And as his senses slowly became adjusted, he was also able to absorb all the abundant sights that filled his wide searching eyes and all the sounds and noises that once again titillated his eardrums. All the familiar magic of this his theatre of dreams was now gradually returning and becoming so familiar to him once more, so much so that he had to figuratively pinch himself to prove that he was actually there on his bench again after an absence of nearly six years.

With an increasing sense of exhilaration now filling the whole of his being he also found that he needed to convince himself that he had ever been away. For it is that very strange phenomena that allows a person to momentarily blank out, as if they had never existed, all the interim years when they find themselves returned to a place of such welcoming and familiar surroundings. And it is exactly what Arthur was experiencing at that moment of euphoria when all the anxieties and traumas of his six years of absence seemed to gradually drain away from his mind and his body, to leave him limply leaning back on his bench. Any passerby that may have taken the time to glance in Arthur's direction could not have failed to notice the somewhat rare, smug expression and air of self satisfaction that was exuding from this rather slight built man who was now back where he knew that he truly belonged.

Sitting there, once again fully in tune with his surroundings and finally convinced that he had truly 'come home' he was able to mull over at length on all that he had seen and heard and experienced and all with a strange glow of personal achievement. And then to reflect even further on the biggest question of anyone who had been subjected to what Arthur had been subjected to, the question of why?.......Why had the world allowed itself to be drawn so close to annihilation, and no matter how hard Arthur turned the question over in his mind, it adamantly chose to remain unresolved.

For nearly five hours he continued to deeply root himself within his thoughts before the clock in his brain indicated that it was time to close down from the mental exertions that he had been demanding from himself with the multitude of questions that he had somehow allowed to pervade his head. This was even after he had promised himself that what had gone was best left behind him, for what was important to him now was what lay ahead and that was something that he had not needed to consider for many a year, with each day and any thoughts beyond that being out of his control whilst he had been in uniform and under orders.

So picking up his raincoat and trilby hat he rose from his bench and walked slowly, yet purposefully out of the station and headed for the address of Mrs Hinchcliffe and her boarding house just off the Hagley Road, where he had rented a room before enlisting into the RAMC. The kindly lady, who had taken something of a shine to Arthur, had promised to look after the leather tool bag, containing the Hornby train set, carved wooden train, cigarette cards and annuals and had also confirmed that if a room was available on his return she would be more than happy for him to have it.

But he was to be disappointed, for the sad news that created him there was that Mrs Hinchcliffe had died on VE night when she had been celebrating with thousands of others in the centre of Birmingham. An army transport lorry, driven by a drunken army driver had ploughed into the group she had been with and Mrs Hinchcliffe, along with two others had been killed outright. Now the house was to be sold but her daughter Doreen, knowing how fond her mother had been of Arthur, generously allowed him to use his old room until he could find something else. Even so, Mrs Hinchcliffe had been good to her word and Arthur was gratefully reunited with his precious leather tool bag and its contents.

Over the next few weeks Arthur was to be confronted with so much change, for not only had he to come to terms with civilian life again, it also meant finding new digs and to securing a job. His previous position as Senior Purchasing and Accounts Controller with Chadwicks Premier Bakeries had gone in March 1941, when it had been targeted by the Luftwaffe.

As a result it now imposed upon him the task of scouring the local newspapers for a position that might suit him and which might not have been snatched up due to the demobilization programme and the increasing volume of ex servicemen. But following a growing and frustrating number of false starts he answered an advertisement in the Birmingham Mail, and was surprised and pleased at knowing his persistence was rewarded when he received a request to attend an interview. And although his letter of application had been just one of so many that he had written, he was a little taken aback to discover that the position on offer was in a shoe shop that had just opened in New Street, the city's bomb damaged but regenerating main shopping area.

Soames Footwear, had been founded in 1863 by Mr Joseph Soames as a quality, handmade shoe and repair business in Leicester, and the subsequent decades up to and into the new century had seen the footwear empire grow with four more large shops throughout Leicestershire. But in 1945 as the war finally came to an end and after much deliberation and debate by the family's senior members, it had been decided to branch out with a fresh venture. And so it had fallen to the founder's grandson Mr Isaac Soames to see the project through to a success, him being the fledgling entrepreneur with the grand ideas who had seen the potential for the new business, especially with the pedigree that the family name carried.

So it was that Arthur, in his newly issued Montague Burton demob suit and with a certain apprehension, presented himself at the sparkling new premises of Soames Footwear. There to be greeted with a firm handshake from Mr Isaac Soames, a man in his early thirties with impeccable dress sense of a tailored fit, light grey, two piece double breasted suit and black patent shoes. And with his tall athletic frame, slick black hair and handsome, square jawed features he had the presence and the appearance of some Hollywood film heartthrob. But it was the genial smile and keen, incisive eyes which impressed Arthur the moment he met this very approachable, albeit successful business man about town.

And in return the young Mr Soames took an instant liking to the small, quiet man who brandished, with a certain amount of subdued pride, his service record and a signed, handwritten commendation letter, which included the personal telephone number from his commanding officer. For even though Arthur had retained his soft spoken, inoffensive manner he had also developed a certain reserved confidence which enabled him to at least carry off the impression of self assertion. His previous inhibitions regarding his diminutive physical stature were now suppressed enough to be almost non-existent and this allowed him to compete from the same starting line in the bustling world of the post war years.

"I take it that you volunteered for the RAMC Mr Wilmot?" questioned Mr Soames as he browsed through the documents Arthur had handed to him.

"That's correct sir," Arthur replied with a determined spark of pride in his voice.

"Good for you I say, Mr Wilmot!" the young businessman beamed with a certain understanding of the spirited resolve it must have taken the little man to find his way into the armed forces. "Jolly good for you.... I was with bomber command myself...but it all leaves a scar on you... does it not?"

"Yes!....Yes indeed it does Mr Soames sir!" was Arthur's somewhat thoughtful response. "I can certainly agree with that."

And so what was to be a formal interview, in fact turned out to be more of a casual conversation and ended with Arthur being offered a position as an assistant in Soames Footwear, New Street, Birmingham. However, it came as something of a surprise to both employer and employee that each left that interview with an impression that something right had come out of it. For Mr Isaac Soames felt he had recognised in Arthur the kind of honesty and reliability that not only he required but which also met the strict principles that the older members of the firm demanded of all those they employed.

Arthur on the other hand had also seen something in his new employer, it was that Mr Isaac Soames was the kind of man that he felt he could work with, as well as work for. Even after the brief interview Arthur sensed that there was a genuine sincerity that lay behind the successful businessman exterior which encouraged him to believe that the future was now looking a little more promising.

Although, at the same time it must be said that each were as different as two people could possibly be and yet each would begin their working relationship from the same stand point of actually liking the other and coupled with that was a mutual admiration that each felt was worthy of nurturing.

Nevertheless, Arthur walked away from Soames Footwear with not only the inkling of a smile gracing his features but with the step of a man that realised he had landed firmly on his two feet and grateful for the good fortune that he knew he had been granted. Saying that it was also typical of the man that even in this moment of something bordering on personal elation that he should still seek out the solitude his soul craved for and where he could just be himself without any interference from anyone else. And so before he caught the tram that would ferry him back to his room at Mrs Hinchcliffes he made one small detour and that was, as always to the bench outside the Refreshment Rooms of Platform 7 of Snow Hill Station.

The next problem for Arthur was the finding of new permanent digs for himself, and this proved to be much more difficult with all the ex servicemen seeking the same kind of accommodation. It was also a very demoralising exercise as he applied for more than thirty vacancies only to be disappointed each time, for they were either too expensive or had already been taken, but there were others that simply did not offer the privacy and solitude that Arthur's nature demanded.

And yet, just as he was about to give up all hope of ever finding anything, fate took a hand and directed him to 17 Oakshott Road, a late Victorian three bedroom semi-detached house situated in the quiet residential suburb of Selly Park. With its front gardens and oak tree lined road it had an ambiance that was instantly appreciated by the digs seeking Arthur. It was also the home of Mrs Clarissa Mary Ansell and her daughter Beatrice Anne.

However, as soon as he walked through the door Arthur was aware of a strange aura that seemed to permeate throughout the whole house. It was a brooding sombreness that engulfed you as soon as you entered and which was emphasised by the distinct and pungent stench of cigarettes, an aroma that was so much in contrast to the homely woodiness of his father's fondly remembered pipe.

But the atmosphere that was being created was something other than what this first impression indicated. Perhaps it was the lack of furniture Arthur thought, perhaps that is what gave it a somewhat unlived in feel to it, or there again it could be the rather heavy moroseness of the landlady and her daughter that caused the oddness of the situation.

For Mrs Ansell was a stout, frumpish woman in her middle fifties with an unkempt perm of greying hair and what appeared to be an ingrained, disapproving scowl on her face. Her eyes, when they looked in the direction of her potential lodger seemed as if they could only focus on him momentarily, before shifting from side to side in their sockets seeking out other points of obscure interest. And when she spoke it seemed to coincide with the erratic eye movements, because the words were fired in short, sharp staccato bursts also.

And yet, the most disconcerting detail was the brown nicotine stain on her top lip, clearly emphasising that she was a very heavy smoker. Although, if Arthur had needed any confirmation of this it was at the conclusion of the short period of the twenty minutes that he was actually in the house, for it was then that Mrs Ansell stubbed out her fourth Woodbine cigarette end and proceeded to light her fifth.

Miss Ansell on the other hand was the opposite, being well into her thirties, tall and willowy with sharp facial features that gave the impression that she was undernourished and had never experienced the pleasure of a smile. Although behind the round, silver framed spectacles there was a brightness in the eyes that seemed to yearn for attention and not the brow beating kind that her mother seemed capable of delivering. And her light brown hair appeared to be of some length, even though it was now woven into two plaits and then knitted into a loose, ornate knot at the nape of her neck.

After the small upstairs room at the back of the house had been inspected, the interview took place in the front sitting room where the overbearing Mrs Ansell and her somewhat subjugated daughter sat side by side on the rather dowdy, well used settee. Two very distinct extremes in a mother and daughter could not be imagined Arthur thought to himself as he sat opposite the pair, briefly outlining who and what he was, whilst making sure it was just enough to secure the room.

It was then Mrs Ansell's turn and fussily correcting her position on the sofa, she bloated herself out with a gush of self importance and began, in her quick fire, annoying manner to put forward the somewhat strict and uncompromising house rules.

"You will be given a key to the back door," she announced. "There will be no visitors, male or female after 6pm..... There will be no food in your room.... and apart from your room and the bathroom on the first floor you will not have access to any other part of the house.... Except that is.....that you will be allowed the use of the kitchen for beverages only..... We do not provide meals and apart from sheets and pillow cases there will no other laundry service..... Rent is twenty five shillings a week to be paid one month in advance....Payable now.... then on this day every four weeks thereafter..... A rent book will be provided..........Is all this to your satisfaction Mr Wilmot?"

Ironically, as Arthur walked away from 17 Oakshott Road it was with an air of satisfaction, for he felt he had stumbled on accommodation that suited the solitude that he so craved for and providing he kept to himself, he need only have contact with Mrs Ansell on one day a month. And as he continued on his way to the main road and the tram stop, he allowed himself something of a brief smile when he considered why no one else had taken the room. For if they had been confronted by the same austere welcome and severe conditions it was no wonder the room had not been snapped up earlier.

iv.
A Foot In The Door

From the outset Arthur was able to settle into a convenient routine that seemed to be completely acceptable to him. Each morning he would leave his Oakshott Road lodgings by seven and travel by tram into Birmingham, where he set himself up for the day with a breakfast of tea and toast at a little cafe a few steps away from Snow Hill Station. At precisely 8.30 he would present himself at the premises of Soames Footwear New Street to help prepare the shop for its 9 o.clock opening.

It was obvious to Mr Isaac Soames from virtually the first day, that what he had found in the small of stature, gently spoken, well mannered Arthur Wilmot was a man of impeccable honesty and moral values. All of which were the sterling Victorian qualities that had been the fundamental basis for the employment of all of the firms staff from its very inception, being instigated by the grandfather, honoured by his sons and which were now maintained by his grandson.

However, the young Mr Soames had never favoured the company policy for the necessity of testing the integrity of those they employed by laying little traps to weed out the weak of character. Ploys such as the simple ruse of leaving a ten shilling note only where the singled out employee would find it, or to seemingly overpay them in their wage packet to see if honesty prevailed and yet, in each case that Arthur was unwittingly subjected to the soundness of his character was shown to be beyond reproach.

And Soames Footwear was not a small shop, for it boasted generous floor space on two levels with Gentlemans, Ladies and Childrens departments. This had been just one of the numerous far reaching initiatives of the young Mr Soames, who had surmounted much hostility from certain elders of the family when he had broached his ideas and proposals to the board of directors. For the whole Soames philosophy and reputation had been built entirely upon handmade, quality footwear.

Even so Mr Soames had successfully argued that to survive in the new post war consumer world of the high street shops, Soames Footwear needed to be in front of the times and not merely moving along with it. And so the shop had become something of a proving ground for him and his progressive approach to the business, and there were those in the family hierarchy who would certainly welcome the fall from grace of the young upstart if his 'mad cap' ideas failed.

As for Arthur, all the way through his working life his natural instinct had dictated that he fully acquainted himself with every aspect of the work he was employed to do. This approach stemmed directly back to the Lamberts little shop and through his time at Chadwicks Premier Bakeries and even with his war service in the RAMC. So it was that he now committed himself to acquire a full knowledge of the footwear business from the traditional manufacturing techniques and styles to the many modern innovations in fashion that were creeping in from abroad. And all this did not go unnoticed by his employer, for within just a few months Mr Soames was finding that he was relying on Arthur more and more, and in recognition he was raised to the position of assistant manager with a very respectable increase in his wages to dignify his responsibilities.

Although the shop was open six days a week, Arthur was allowed a half day off on Thursday afternoons. It was then that he was able to leave his work firmly behind the doors of Soames Footwear and escape for a few hours to his one place of refuge, the bench outside the Refreshment Rooms on Platform 7 of Snow Hill Station. It was there that his mind was able to clear itself of all the tediousness of everyday life and he could just concentrate on his one real passion, that of watching the world pass him by from his well established vantage point.

So life for Arthur had a kind of perfection to it. He had a job that not only suited his personality, it was for an employer that he liked and respected and the room that he rented was in a household that certainly did not bother the solitude he yearned for at the end of each day. Thus, within these confines he was able to develop a well structured routine for himself, which saw him leaving his room by seven in the morning and never returning any later than nine in the evening, six days a week.

The routine also meant that every Monday morning he would remove the sheets from his bed, along with his towel and leave them folded on the chair outside the door to his room and on his return in the evening he would find clean ones waiting for him. The only time he entered the kitchen was in the mornings on his way through to the back door and then on his return in the evening, when he would fill his thermos flask with tea to take to his room, his little private haven, his retreat where he would read his Railway magazines or the book that he would borrow from the library. Or he would just sit and allow his mind to wander out through the window and across the gardens and the rooftops of the other houses and just float away in contemplative meditation of the night sky.

Or sometimes, he would take the leather tool bag from the bottom of his wardrobe and wistfully browse through its contents, simply remembering exactly what each item meant to him. The Boys Own Annuals that he had read from cover to cover, the Hornby clockwork railway set with its circle of track that his parents had saved for months to buy him for his twelfth birthday. And then there was the little wooden engine, painted black that his father had made for him and the cigarette cards with pictures of famous railway engines. All this was so much a part of his past that had been shared so lovingly with Charlotte his sister and what he now considered as his own private sanctum.

However it was a sanctum that he suspected had been broached, even within his first week at 17 Oakshott Road. It had been the methodical side to Arthur's nature that had realised the contents of his so precious leather tool bag had been tampered with. It was only a small thing, but in Arthur's mind the thought that either his landlady or her daughter had even touched those such treasured items made him feel to some extent that his privacy had been violated, which was something he had never experienced at Mrs Hinchcliffe's.

Arthur had realised from the outset that he could not prevent this kind of surreptitious meddling in his personal life but he could and did take early measures to at least thwart the possibility of any mail being tampered with. As a consequence he approached the tobacconist newsagent near Snow Hill Station, where he bought his newspapers and Railway Magazine from and who also advertised an accommodation address service. And so for sixpence a week, what mail he was likely to receive was delivered to the shop where it was kept for him to collect.

But this had been the only real blip in what Arthur came to consider as an otherwise acceptable situation with each day fitting neatly into each week and each week fitting into each month. When, as arranged every fourth Saturday evening without fail, he would knock on the front sitting room door and hand over five pounds, have his rent book signed and all without a word being spoken by either party.

This routine also extended to another corner of Arthur's somewhat enigmatic nature and frugal needs when every Thursday afternoon, on his way to Snow Hill Station he would deposit a portion of his wages into a savings account at Lloyds Bank, thus adding to the very sizable unspent pay that had been accumulated from his war service days. For Arthur had never yielded to alcohol or tobacco and had never indulged in any kind of social activities to warrant wasteful spending, even as a release from the stresses of his time in those wartime years. This was just another aspect to Arthur's reclusive world, but which had led to a very respectable position being gained through financial stability.

And so the years slipped by and the new decade of the fifties filtered in and found Arthur still with Soames Footwear in New Street Birmingham but now as its manager and well respected by his employers and his staff alike.

The new decade also saw Arthur still a lodger at 17 Oakshott Road, and apart from the fact that his rent had increased sharply from twenty five shillings to two pounds two shillings a week nothing else in Arthur's life had really changed which was most agreeable to his quiet, unassuming nature. It was also a measure of the contentment that Arthur felt about his life that he had never even contemplated making any moves to alter it.

But changes were about to happen which would be the catalyst of events that would shape the rest of his life and they began early in the year of 1952, as the nation mourned the sad passing of its monarch King George the Sixth.

Right from his first week at Oakshott Road it had been Arthur's habit each Sunday, to leave his digs by nine o clock in the morning and travel by tram to the cemetery at Hockley, where he would spend a few minutes at the graves of his father and mother and then half an hour or even more at the grave side of his beloved sister Charlotte. It had always been something of a pilgrimage for Arthur since his sister's untimely death and had only been interrupted by his wartime service years. For it was there, looking down on the simple inscription of his sister's name and dates that he would unburden himself of all those things that he would have shared with his sister if she had survived the tuberculosis, simply for the comfort and peace of mind that she could give him.

But in the real world that he now lived in, there was no one in whom he could confide, although it was his choice to keep that real world at bay without allowing any glimpse or chink of himself ever being visible. For it had been Charlotte who had really known and understood all the complex frailties of Arthur's inner secret self, all the doubts and prevailing fears that he had carried with him through his childhood and into adolescence and which Charlotte had taken with her to her grave. And more often than not, the small leather envelope containing the precious lock of silky auburn hair that could glint with golden strands in the sunlight, would find its way from Arthur's inside pocket, to leave him musing even more deeply, with the softness of its touch on his delicately probing finger.

But he would walk away from that grave side with something of a lightness of heart, merely because he had been given the opportunity to silently converse with such a freeness of thought that he consciously deprived himself of in his every day contacts.

From the cemetery he would catch a tram to his next important destination, his other haven on Platform 7. There he would have his Sunday lunch in the Refreshment Rooms and while away the afternoon quietly observing all the fascinating shadowy forms that passed before him, wondering who they were and where they were going. And a question that would often form in his mind while contemplating each of those fleeting images was, just how many thousands had actually passed him by and that he had watched from that bench over his forty or so years.

And following his vigil, he would wend his thoughtful way back to Oakshott Road by his self regulated time of eight o clock, to once again closet himself away in his room with a sense of being revitalised and ready to face the coming week.

v.

Winds of Change

However, it was on a Sunday morning early in the spring of 1952 as Arthur was passing the front sitting room of 17 Oakshott Road on his way to catch one of the new buses that were now superseding the trams, when the door suddenly swung open to reveal Mrs Ansell standing there. For a moment Arthur was somewhat taken aback by this daunting, unscheduled appearance of his landlady, who stood with such a broad smile adorning her face and the inevitable cigarette in her raised chubby, nicotine browned fingers.

To Arthur it was a rather incongruous and artificial smile from a person who, over the years he had only really come into contact with on a monthly basis so as to pay his rent. But now he was completely shaken by her abrupt and certainly out of character appearance. Even so it was the contrived and overly pleasant manner of the words that she spoke that really brought the defensive shields instantly up inside his head.

"Ah!... I'm glad I caught you Mr Wilmot!" she announced with the smile so tightly drawn across her face that it seemed to Arthur to be more like some grotesque gargoyle mask. "It's my daughter Beatrice," she continued, "it's her birthday today and....well!.... we'd like you to join us for a small celebration tea this evening."

If you had said to Arthur that somehow the earth had stopped spinning and he was now floating, mindless in the void of space with all his senses and perceptions on hold he would not have been anymore surprised. Speechless and motionless he stood with his mouth opening and shutting with absolutely no sound whatsoever coming to the surface.

"That's if it's convenient to you of course Mr Wilmot?" she continued with a fawning tilt of her head. "So.... shall we say six?"

And with that and still with the sickly smile etched deep into her cheeks she turned back into the sitting room, closing the door behind her.

Arthur could not say how long he remained glued to the hall floor in a completely astonished and dumbfounded state of mind, for he was not used to this kind of unsolicited invitation, especially after so many years of having such limited contact. But finally, he gathered his puzzled thoughts together and very slowly turned and made his way towards the back door, trying desperately to rationalise what this totally unexpected summons actually meant.

And later at the cemetery over his sister's grave, he stood for almost an hour in the drizzling rain with the small leather envelope in his fingers, inwardly discussing the words Mrs Ansell had spoken and all the possible implications that went with them. Even as he boarded the bus to Snow Hill Station he was still very bemused and equally very disturbed. For the one definite conclusion that he managed to come to terms with, was that his self induced, yet comfortable isolation was now in imminent danger of being seriously undermined.

All through the afternoon his mind was in turmoil with every miniscule detail of his encounter with his landlady and the thought of what was to come, which made the bench outside the Refreshment Rooms on Snow Hill Station rather uncomfortable indeed. He had always tried to avoid casual conversation with people and as a consequence he had never mastered any of the accepted social arts. Although from what he had so far been able to discern regarding his landlady and her daughter, he doubted if they were very proficient in those skills either. He also realised there was no common ground for either himself or the two women to establish any possible rapport and he also doubted whether he could be interesting enough to provide stimulating conversation. And as the hours slowly passed those questions ground deep into his mind.

But dutifully at six o clock, he found himself seated at the rear parlour dining table with a ration defying celebration tea spread out before him and being volubly fussed over by the combined ministrations of Mrs Ansell and her daughter Beatrice. He should not have worried about providing idle chit chat for that was taken care of, predominately by his landlady who talked about everything but nothing at all and as always with the incessant cigarette either in her podgy fingers or dangling from her lips. It was clear that the austere existence that she and her daughter resided in had given her a very narrow view of the outside world. And yet, occasionally small snippets of information did seep through the otherwise inane torrent of gossipy nonsense for Arthur to piece together and then to form something of a background to his landlady.

Apparently Mr Bertram Ansell had owned two rather classy restaurants and had died of a heart attack in 1936. After all the debts and mortgages had been paid off, Mrs Ansell had sold up and with the residue and the sizable insurance payout had supported herself and her daughter ever since. It was also very obvious from the one sided conversation that neither, Mrs Ansell or Beatrice had ever worked for a living, being totally reliant on Mr Ansell in all things, before and after his death. And apart from these few specific details that Arthur was able to pick up on and file away in his head, he could honestly admit that so much more of his landlady's verbal onslaught had been nothing but mindless, unimportant drivel and had been lost on Arthur completely.

So it was, with the memory of the rigid smiles and harsh tones of Mrs Ansell's voice, combined with the uncomfortable stuttering of her daughter, that Arthur finally took to his room an hour and a half later. And sitting in the only arm chair that his room possessed, he gazed out through his window at the dimming light of the night sky and took a deep, thoughtful breath to ponder heavily on the question of what it all meant. But the most serious thought came with the realisation that his so well preserved defences of his inner self had now at least been partially breached.

However, what was to come next was a course of actions that Arthur seemed powerless to do anything about. It was to be a process that was slow and yet methodical on the part of Mrs Ansell and her daughter, but it was to be very effective.

From that Sunday onwards it became expected that Arthur would return to the house by six o clock in the evening to share tea time with Mrs Ansell and Beatrice. No matter what he said or did to excuse himself from what he deemed to be totally invasive on his private life, was either dismissed out of hand or simply fell onto stony ground. For Mrs Ansell's attitude was very insistent, saying that she had already bought the cold meat for the weekend, or that Beatrice had baked a cake specially and she even used the rather lame ploy that she wanted to make sure that Arthur was eating properly. The most surprising factor that tormented Arthur's mind was that at no point was it even hinted that he should surrender his ration book to augment the tea table.

It was also increasingly clear that Mrs Ansell was very persuasive and adept at aiming her reasons specifically at the conscience of her lodger to get her own way, knowing full well that his seemingly honourable nature would direct him never to offend with a refusal. And it also became noticeable to Arthur that the jittery eye affliction of his landlady, that had been so apparent at his initial interview, only seemed to affect her when she was in a position of being overly forthright when pressing home her will on him. So it was that Arthur needed all his inherent good manners to come to the fore and with a courteous smile accept the inevitable with a polite bow of the head.

And the strange behaviour of his landlady and her daughter continued, for it came to be quite a regular occurrence to find Mrs Ansell or Beatrice or both fussing about in the kitchen when Arthur came in of an evening. They would bid him a somewhat over genial 'Good evening' and smile their tight smiles and Arthur would hastily fill his thermos flask with tea before nervously bidding them a 'Good night' as he retreated to his room.

So many other little modifications were now seeping into Arthur's quiet, unassuming way of life that they seemed to defy any kind of rational behaviour. Like the time that he found bright new chintzy curtains hanging at the window of his room, replacing the aging mothy ones that had previously hung there. Fortunately they did not deprive him of his view of the garden and the sky above the surrounding houses, even though the gaudy colours were certainly not to his simple, reserved tastes. It was also becoming the norm to find a handful of flowers from the garden, neatly arranged in a vase on the sideboard next to his bed.

But the instance that capped it all off for Arthur, was when he returned to Oakshott Road on one particular Monday evening, to discover Beatrice in his room making his bed. It had always been the accepted house rule that he should strip the sheets and pillow case off his bed in the morning and for them to be replaced by clean ones. So with a certain subdued twinge of annoyance, Arthur tactfully remained in the open doorway, waiting and watching as Beatrice carefully completed her task. Then with a polite 'Thank you' and a respectful bow of his head he allowed her tall, slender form to pass, as the merest hint of lavender teased his nostrils. And as she disappeared down the stairs Arthur leant heavily against the door frame and sighed such a bitter sigh that seemed to encapsulate the whole creeping sense of violation he was feeling.

However, these adjustments to his long standing routine were in themselves small and insignificant and hardly worth a mention. And yet, to place them and all the other inexplicable and unnerving twists and turns into the context of this previously austere household, only made the whole baffling situation in need of a clearer explanation.

Arthur was now becoming evermore concerned and perplexed at this curious reversal to the previously strict and rigid regime that he had neatly fitted into and which had suited his solitary life style. In fact he was finding the newly imposed situation a complete intrusion without any tangible reason being given and Arthur's rather trusting innocence did not allow him to construe any really devious intent in any of it. Even when on one Sunday teatime, he had unwittingly brought into the one sided conversation a reference to the sharp increase that had been made to his rent. For a brief moment something of an embarrassing silence had settled over the rear parlour dining table, with Arthur inwardly suspecting that he may somehow have overstepped the mark. But then with a fleeting, almost imperceptible eye contact being exchanged between mother and daughter, Mrs Ansell had replied in a strangely soft, condescending tone.

"It's the war Mr Wilmot…..since the war the cost of everything has risen so much….and believe me… I do feel guilty about asking for the extra…That's why I hope that all the…. little….. considerations ….the curtains and the flowers and the such… will be looked on as a small gesture on my part…. to at least… make your stay with us….a little more agreeable."

And as quickly as the subject had been raised and dealt with, Mrs Ansell had managed to astutely turn the conversation around from money issues, to much more mundane matters. But even as she had blustered on down her different path of nonsense chatter, Arthur had found himself brooding momentarily on the little hiatus he had caused in the conversation, but it was short lived before the incessant sound of his landlady's grating voice had obliterated any possible suspicions that he may have been forming.

And yet, it was in the quiet, precious moments in the late evenings, cloistered away in his room, mulling over the intricacies of his thoughts and those parts of his life that had a real and profound meaning to him, that Arthur now found were being infiltrated by having to analyse the motives behind all the strange happenings at 17 Oakshott Road. This dilemma was even denying him the comfort and contentment of mind he derived from watching the world pass by as he sat on the bench outside the Refreshment Rooms of Platform 7. For now instead of his normal bland, inscrutable expression, there always seemed to be a deep concerned furrow pervading his brow to reflect the direction his heavy thoughts were taking him.

But the most perturbing development transpired two months after the first Sunday invitation to join Mrs Ansell and Beatrice for tea. Again Arthur dutifully returned at the agreed time, to be seated at the rear parlour table where he was presented with another spread of tea time delicacies. He endured the fussing females attentions and then gave his thanks for an enjoyable meal and leant back in his chair to wait for Mrs Ansell to delve into her usual hour and half of unstoppable, one sided discourse. But this time she decided to make a strange and totally unexpected suggestion.

"Perhaps we could make you a little more comfortable Mr Wilmot!" she said smiling that moronic and insincere smile.

And with that Arthur was ushered into the front sitting room, the room he had not seen, let alone been given permission to enter since his first interview. It was then somehow contrived that he should be placed at one end of the small settee that occupied the centre of the room, and that Beatrice, under her mother's guidance was seated next to him.

"Oh this is pleasant.....Arthur!" Mrs Ansell enthused with that inane smile still creasing her face. "You have no objections to us calling you by your first name I take it?"

Arthur made no objection, although he could not have done even if he had wanted to, for he seemed to be in something very close to a state of shock.

"This is nice," Mrs Ansell continued. "Don't you agree Arthur?"

Again he made no comment other than a small nod of his head for he was still struggling with this flood of amiability.

"Oh this really is nice Arthur," she glowed once more. "And Beatrice so likes you being here....Don't you dear?"

Arthur quickly glanced to his right and just caught a glimpse of a demure lift of the eyes behind the silver framed spectacles, as something resembling a smile chased briefly across Beatrice's rather pleasant features. It suddenly crossed his mind that this was the very first time that he had seen her really smile and not the merest flicker of the cheeks that he had witnessed over the last few months.

"Oh yes... I do mother!" she cooed obediently. "I do!"

This was all too cloying for words Arthur thought to himself. He was not a sociable person by nature and the close proximity of these two women was making him feel very uncomfortable in deed. It was not in his character to make idle conversation and certainly not in this kind of informal situation and so every minute that he had to endure it made the need to excuse himself ever more vital. Then just as he was about to express his polite thanks and to take his leave, Mrs Ansell seemed to pre-empt what he was intending to do.

"I'm sure you'd like another cup of tea Arthur," she said raising herself out of her chair. "You talk to Beatrice..... and I won't be two ticks!"

And she was gone, leaving behind her a beating silence between two people who had absolutely nothing to say to each other. Arthur now sat without any recognisable impulse to initiate even a casual exchange with Beatrice, for in the past whenever he had been confronted with the need to pass a few moments of convivial conversation with someone he had either dried up almost immediately or developed an embarrassed cough to excuse himself from continuing.

It also seemed to Arthur that Beatrice was suffering from the same tongue tied affliction, for she now sat staring into the few flickering flames that danced amongst the coals in the fire grate. However Arthur did manage a fleeting glance in her direction and came to the conclusion that her taciturn manner was simply because she had never been given any occasions to mix with her own kind and age group, this being a consequence of the overpowering presence of her mother.

So merely because of the fact that both Arthur and Beatrice were incapable of the simple skills involved in conversation, all that remained between them was an embarrassing and pulsating hush with each just waiting for the agony to end. Even so, because it seemed that they were both damned by the same ailment, Arthur was now feeling a strange sensation of empathy towards Beatrice. This was a feeling that he had never experienced before and he was unsure of what it was trying to tell him and equally what to do about it, to either quell it or to find a way to cope with it.

There was also a strange sense of warmth towards her, which was now being kindled as his nose once again detected the subtle fragrance of lavender. He easily recognised this from the sweet scented aromas that tended to drift up from the flower seller stall outside the gates of Hockley Cemetery on his Sunday visits to the gravesides of his parents and especially Charlotte.

He stole one more glance in the direction of Beatrice and to his surprise he found her glancing towards him. There was an exchange of smiles, only this time the smile on Beatrice's face held something more of a coy cordiality to it which caused Arthur's gaze to linger on it that few seconds longer.

Fortunately it was just then that Mrs Ansell came clattering in with a tray.

vi.
Duplicity

Later that evening, Arthur sat on the side of his bed in his darkened room staring out of his window at the scar like crescent moon in the clear night sky. In the palm of his hand was the small envelope containing his sister's auburn lock of hair and with his fore finger probing gently inside he touched the soft silky strands, seeking the comfort they always seemed to offer him. He would often just sit with the light out simply musing at the ever changing starry heavens, whilst inwardly he would ponder over the events of the day and prepare himself for the one to come. Sometimes it would be well into the early hours before he stretched out on his bed to doze until his alarm clock again summoned him to full wakefulness.

But tonight the musing was taking a more profound direction, because tonight he was striving to deal with the question of exactly what the unfamiliar sensation he was experiencing really meant. For he could not get out of his mind the smile that he had shared with Beatrice, before it was interrupted by her mother's entrance. To Arthur, it seemed to have been a moment of shared empathy and mutual understanding between them and as he continued to gaze out into the night sky he wondered and strangely hoped that it had been the same for Beatrice.

Long into the silent hours before the morning light began to tinge the roof tops of the houses, he sat in a quiet meditation of where life was taking him. Until this moment in time he had been content with what it had given him, never expecting anything more than what he was prepared to give back and this had been his simple philosophy for survival, and it was with these thoughts teasing his mind that he finally succumbed to sleep.

However, over the next few weeks it appeared to Arthur that a new phase had begun in his life, for something that had remained dormant inside him had now been stirred and he was striving to understand it. He was now actually timing his departure in the morning and his arrival back at night in the hope of an encounter with Beatrice and an exchange of more shy smiles. It was also more than a coincidence that Beatrice always seemed to be making his bed when he came back on a Monday evening. And he would know she was in his room before he entered, simply because of the feint fragrance of lavender that reached his searching nostrils as he topped the stairs to the landing.

The same could also be said about Sunday's, for it had become a regular feature for Arthur and Beatrice to be left alone in the sitting room while Mrs Ansell made the tea. Equally the time it was taking her to complete the task seemed to take longer each week.

There was also a guarded sweetness about Beatrice that was somehow endearing, even to Arthurs innocence in such matters. And this was becoming more evident and disarming with each Sunday evening that they shared together, with the conversation between these two normally shy and retiring people developing beyond mere embarrassed pleasantries to a more relaxed exchange of mutually stimulating themes. However, this only seemed to be apparent when the dominant mother was not in the room to interfere.

And somewhat oddly, this new phase was not a displeasing one for Arthur and over the ensuing weeks his vigils on the bench outside the Refreshment Rooms on Platform 7 took on a completely new and fresh horizon for him. Gone was the questioning nature of his thoughts, gone was the morose and tainted reflections on his past and what lay for him in the future. And even the previous daunting question of the seven inch height difference between himself and Beatrice had somehow dulled into insignificance.

To Arthur the future now seemed brighter than it had ever done before and that future revolved around his deepening thoughts about Beatrice. Without any effort he was now beginning to sense a warmth in his heart whenever she crept into his mind and this would be wherever he might be at any given moment. It was a sensation that Arthur had never felt before and as a consequence of his reticent disposition there was also an accompanying mistrust of that which he did not understand.

Even so, the full implications of this growing intimacy were profoundly identified for Arthur one Sunday evening with a seemingly casual comment by Mrs Ansell. As usual she entered the sitting room with her tray of tea things and stopped, looking first at Arthur and then to her daughter and then back to Arthur again.

"Oh..... you do make a lovely couple," she fawned gushingly with such a broad smile adorning her face.

The words promptly resounded around inside Arthur's head, almost to the point of making him feel dizzy with the suggestion that they were making. For up until that moment he had never even considered Beatrice and himself as being looked on as a 'couple' and it completely unsettled him, even though he was coming to the conclusion that he was developing a curious but definite affection for his landlady's daughter. But for it to mature beyond that was completely against Arthur's innate need for solitude, and equally he was also mindful that it would mean a commitment to another person and that sudden deduction flashed like a bolt of lightning through his head to instantly become a disconcerting factor, producing so many qualms and misgivings.

For there was an unswerving honesty about Arthur that was respected by all he had ever come into contact with. And if it was that Beatrice believed that she might have expectations with regards to their common future together, then he must blame only himself for creating that situation. But to think that Mrs Ansell might be looking favourably in that direction also merely added to the conundrum for Arthur to ponder on.

What followed was a somewhat embarrassing few minutes, in which all conversation ceased within an awkward, brooding silence as the tea was poured out and drank. Arthur was now fully aware that the amiable atmosphere had changed and there was now a definable chill in the room that he felt only he could have induced. For the pointed few words that Mrs Ansell had uttered were still ringing loudly in his head and for some reason they were disturbing him greatly. And to make things worse, scrutinizing expressions had appeared on the faces of the two women, which he tried desperately to ignore. But this only made Arthur fidget more uncomfortably on his seat, and with his normally iron reserve somehow ineffective he lowered his head, not knowing where else to look.

Suddenly, it all got too much for him and slowly getting to his feet he sheepishly made his way to the door, all the time imagining that two pairs of eyes were now burning deep into his back. And reaching the door he stood for a moment with his hand on the brass knob, feeling decidedly awkward and out of place. Then with his eyes still staring sightless at the floor, he half turned towards the two women and politely thanked them for a pleasant evening, before making a rather hurried escape.

However, it was not until he was standing in the hallway outside the sitting room that he fully realised just how much the few words that Mrs Ansell had spoken had affected him. And it came as quite a shock to him when he caught sight of a face in the hallstand mirror, a face that was unrecognisable at first, being grey and drawn and completely drained of all its usual colour. And even as he stood there, deeply challenged by the reflected image in the mirror and desperately trying to compose himself back to his habitually unflinching, emotionless demeanour, he sensed that something with far reaching consequences had taken place in the front sitting room just a few moments before, something that was now out of his hands, out of his control.

And later still, in his own room he had much to occupy his crowded, fretful mind as he once again contemplated the darkness of the night sky beyond his window.

But as far as Mrs Ansell and Beatrice were concerned, the impression they maintained over the subsequent weeks was as if nothing out of the ordinary had occurred and gradually life at 17 Oakshott Road dropped back into the old pattern of the previous routine. And Arthur was quite content that this should be so, for his whole inhibited nature had been sorely undermined by what those few simple words expressed by Mrs Ansell had really hinted at, and which had left him with a lingering sense of disquiet and unsettling concerns.

Be that as it may, a seed had been sewn and over the next few weeks that seed began to germinate in Arthur's brain producing something of a flowering of hesitant acceptance. The seed was in fact the few words that had been meticulously well phrased so as to be planted in Arthur's mind as part of a carefully manoeuvred process on the part of the landlady and her daughter, just a few supposedly innocent words spoken in such a light friendly manner that could not possibly be misconstrued as anything other than innocuous. And yet in reality they were words that began to worm away beneath the resilient defences that Arthur tended to construct around himself.

In every respect, what was now happening must be viewed as resembling the analogy of the spider and the fly and like the fly, Arthur was being drawn further and further into the web. For it was his intrinsic naivety in such matters of the heart that were to be his undoing against the wiles of this manipulating pair and their well devised scheme of duplicity.

As a consequence something very profound began to simmer in this shy, introverted man who had never been prone to exhibit any sign of sentimental weakness in the past, but the strange, involuntary feelings caused him to question every aspect of his personality. It was as if the words had opened a doorway into Arthur's heavily defended inner self, thus easing a way through to remove any remaining opposition that may exist to prevent him from changing the way he viewed his life.

So when that so significant statement 'You do make a lovely couple!' was repeated one Sunday evening a month or so later, Arthur found that his normally well grounded sense of reasoning wavered badly, almost as if some lucky blow had caught him off guard and he was reeling back with the full implications of what the words were actually inferring. And the strange part was that his deep seated resolve was not fighting or resisting anymore and he found himself being drawn, almost mechanically to glance hopefully towards Beatrice. She in turn responded with such an enticing and affectionate smile while offering a demurely, outstretched hand seeking Arthur's hand to hold.

It was such an irresistible gesture to Arthur that he was now totally defenceless to resist.

And that was it...The die was cast! ...There was now no retreat!... No going back!

What followed for Arthur was a whirlwind of unrecognisable emotions, emotions that were carried along on an unstoppable flood tide which was not within his control or his making. As a result it was as if he instantly became a spectator to the ensuing conversation between Mrs Ansell and her daughter and which seemed to drift all around him and beyond his scope of comprehension, leaving him to either nod or mutter some incoherent and nonsensical response.

Even so, short but distinct phrases just managed to permeate through the density of his dulled perceptions, phrases that Arthur's senses were telling him that much was being assumed, but they were phrases which he seemed unable to either contribute to or even contradict.

Phrases such as...

"You seem to be so content in each other's company!" and

"It would be lovely to have Arthur in the family!" and

"There would be so much to organise!" and even,

"Perhaps we could have the King Charles Hotel for the reception?"

But they were phrases that fortunately seemed to stop just short of actually naming the day. Even so, when Arthur finally retreated to his room that night, dazed and dumbfounded, they were just a few phrases amongst so many more that he was able to reflect on, that seemed to imply that somehow before he had left the front sitting room he had tentatively become engaged to Beatrice. And this was without the merest glimmer of a memory of an actual proposal on his part ever being made.

So it was that a very confused Arthur rested his head on his pillow in the early hours of the morning to yield to an uneasy sleep, for now the strict moral code of the man to do the correct thing seemed to be in mortal conflict with that which resisted any form of closeness with another person. All of his life Arthur had meticulously fought hard never to allow his defences to lapse for a single minute, always aware of the consequences that any weakness on his part might have. And yet the inherent honesty of the man, the well cultivated honourable nature that he had a quiet, unassuming pride in, was now in danger of being seriously compromised.

Even so, it was the honourable nature in Arthur that the conniving Mrs Ansell and her daughter were now relying upon to do the right thing.

vii.
Harold Morris

It was the next morning, the Monday morning that Arthur was reminded beyond any remaining doubt of the events of the previous evening. For as he was making his way to the back entrance, the door to the front sitting room swung open midst a billowing cloud of eye stinging tobacco smoke and Mrs Ansell appeared, fist erect with her Woodbine pointing skywards and wearing that broad, fatuous smile that seemed to envelope the whole of her face.

"Good morning Arthur," she announced beaming widely. "Perhaps now that you're joining the family.... it would be better if you used the front door."

And with that she took a long satisfied pull on her cigarette before sliding back inside and closing the door behind her.

Arthur stood speechless for a long moment just staring at the closed sitting room door, trying to smother the inferno that those few words had ignited in his mind. He fully understood what had been said and he even managed to file it within the context of the events of the night before but his natural resistance was not allowing him to come to terms with all the complications the logical side of his brain was forming. And still very thoughtful he slowly turned away and obediently walked out through the front door of the house, realising as he did that this was simply for the neighbours and appearances only.

It had seemed to be such a surreal statement that the landlady had made and yet the truth of it burned within him during the whole of the bus journey into Birmingham. Even as he ate his breakfast in the little cafe, his head still buzzed with those words, while trying desperately to rearrange them to mean something completely different, but in that exercise he failed miserably. It was as if he was actually shutting out the true relevance of the whole situation he was being confronted by.

He went through the rest of the day in something of a robotic trance, for his duties were so well defined that in some respect he was able to perform them without too much thought. Even so there were a number of occasions that he caught Mr Soames watching him and it was in the late afternoon that his employer finally enquired as to his welfare.

"You look rather abstracted today Arthur!" he said in a concerned manner. "Is there anything I can do to help?"

Arthur made some vague reference to repairs that needed doing at his lodgings, before thanking Mr Soames for his kindly offer, for there was no way he was going to admit to the fact that he was to marry his landlady's daughter, as that would have been an unthinkable admission to make, but why?

That night Arthur was later than usual returning to 17 Oakshott Road, for it was well after ten when he opened the door to his little sanctuary and sank into his armchair to ponder the darkened sky beyond his window. So much had been occupying his thoughts all day long and he had felt that he needed the bench outside the Refreshment Rooms on Platform 7 for a few precious hours of untroubled, detached peace of mind. But that was not to be, for he had been unable to free himself of the scathing inner scrutiny that his brooding thoughts were demanding of him. And the depth of those thoughts was to such an extent, that his beloved engines came and went completely unnoticed by him, as did all the interweaving, anonymous forms that normally fascinated him so much.

For just by taking away the shock and the speed of events, one side of him was actually viewing the idea of marriage to Beatrice in a favourable manner but at the same time his natural timidity and need for solitude placed the whole notion into the absurd category. And considering all the pros and the cons, the confusion of his thoughts only left him even more bewildered.

As a married man his whole life would have to alter and yet it was not as if he did not find Beatrice unattractive. In fact, even as he sat there on his bench he was able to conjure up her features, the fineness of her cheeks, the primness of her lips and the sparkle of her brown eyes, even the depth of the brown in her long hair that was always contained in plaits and then into varying styles around and over her head, that would change daily. Ironically this and the slenderness of her form only seemed to add to her height, leaving Arthur to briefly consider the good seven inch difference there was in his bride to be. But he was able to quickly shake this fact away for he did not allow it to bother him anymore.

From what he had managed to gather during his stumbling conversations with his 'fiancé' it was clear at least that they did have one thing in common, in that she had led a very sheltered and isolated existence albeit beneath the strict and dominant control of her mother. So in that respect Arthur thought, they would both have the same difficulties with regards to sharing their lives together, although it has to be said, that Arthur had fervently believed that he would never marry and that he would die a bachelor and alone. That said, the mere thought of marriage, of actually committing his life to another person had been so far removed from what he thought his future was to be, that now he had to seriously consider the prospect, it felt like a very unnerving and daunting proposition indeed.

But it is also a measure of the honesty and integrity of the man that although he had numerous misgivings about his future with Beatrice, he also felt he was now somehow honour bound to see it through and to make sure that his wife wanted for nothing in his care. However, the one thing that his extended thinking had not taken into consideration was the fact that there had been no indication so far, that the happy couple should live anywhere other than 17 Oakshott Road.

And as he sat in the darkness of his room contemplating the moonlight on the rooftops through his window he had a sudden regret pierce his sanguine mood and that was the agonising thought of having to forfeit completely his need for this kind of solitude.

Over the next six weeks, it seemed to Arthur as if he was trapped upon a speeding rollercoaster of perplexing emotions that took him to extreme highs and lows in dizzying succession, even though at no point with him actually being consulted with regards to anything to do with the forthcoming arrangements. Except that is, to when it came to the cost of it all, for more and more he was being confronted by Mrs Ansell for money to pay bills, that he never actually had sight of but which seemed to mount up on a daily basis.

In due course however, he was officially informed that it was to be a very quiet ceremony at the local registry office, but Mrs Ansell needed a complete new outfit and a hat as did Beatrice and each needed visits to the hairdressers, not to mention the compulsory purchase of a ring. There were to be four taxis for the few friends and neighbours that were to be invited and the day would be rounded off with a buffet reception at the King Charles Hotel's side function room.

All of this and many more areas of expense seemed to grind agonisingly on Arthur's normally frugal needs. Although, the one saving grace to this growing expenditure was that it was never mentioned or considered by either Beatrice or her mother that Arthur should purchase or hire a suit for himself and this tacit agreement was very agreeable to the reluctant bridegroom.

The Sunday tea time arrangements were still maintained with the primary subject being the wedding and of how happy Arthur would be to have a wife like Beatrice. And slowly over the course of the weeks he somehow came to accept the inevitability of the situation, whilst candidly admitting to himself that he had become quite fond of his bride to be. Even so, was that enough for him to take that one giant plunge into marriage, a marriage that had never even crossed his mind until that fateful Sunday, when Mrs Ansell had spoken those so neatly contrived, yet provocative words, 'Oh... you do make a lovely couple,' merely to coax along Arthurs interest in her daughter, or so he had tentatively come to suspect.

But now midst all the flurry and excitement generated by the two women and their arrangements for the wedding, any doubts Arthur may have been harbouring seemed to lose their significance as he was swept along with the flowing tide of nonsensical feminine chatter. Although when the subject of guests was raised, Arthur did manage to avoid any form of discussion regarding his own list, by implying that he had no living relatives to lay claim to and that Saturday's at Soames Footwear were too busy to allow for more than one employee to be off at any one time. As a result of this the elderly widower Mr Appleby, a slight nodding acquaintance of Arthur's from three doors down was nominated by Mrs Ansell to fulfil the role of best man.

The truth of the matter was, that although Arthur was aware that his father had been born in Cradley Heath, a small town in the

Black Country, sadly no other mention of either of his parents family's background or relatives, living or dead, had ever been made or alluded to. It was also a fact that Arthur's colleagues and even Mr Soames himself, were totally unaware of Arthur's marriage arrangements, a detail that he was determined they should remain in total ignorance of. It is also important to know that he deliberately omitted to mention any reference to his coming wedding when he was confronted with the necessity to request a Saturday off from his employer.

And yet, all this only epitomised the very cautious part to Arthur's nature which tended to draw him to one side, when out of the direct influence of Mrs Ansell or Beatrice, and whisper into his listening ear and remind him of all the subconscious misgivings that were festering away inside his head, misgivings that he would inwardly express to his sister Charlotte, on his weekly visits to her graveside on a Sunday morning. It was there that he would strive to hear her silent words in reply and where, with the small leather envelope containing the lock of her hair touching his trembling fingers, he would stand absorbed in the comfort that it gave him.

Though now the only conclusion that he was able to rationally come to terms with, was that the marriage vows, to an honourable man were there 'until death do you part.' And whenever those words manifested themselves in his thoughts, he was always left to feverishly try and place some subliminal interpretation on them. But it was always to no avail, unless that is, that they held some kind of prophetic significance for him, some kind of omen.

But, the most significant facet to reflect Arthur's deepening qualms was when he took a very decisive action and if someone had asked him why he had taken it, he would not have been able to give them any form of logical response. It was a decision that he had mulled over at every moment that his mind had been clear of any other usurping interference.

So after much consideration Arthur withdrew his savings out of Lloyds Bank, leaving only a moderate one hundred pounds. He then quite deliberately opened a savings account at a Barclays Bank under the assumed name of Harold Edward Morris. It had been much easier than he thought, perhaps because of the very sizable amount of the deposit he made. He was even very careful of making sure that the only address that was given in his application was the newsagents where all his post was already being delivered to.

This simple sly manoeuvre was completely out of character for Arthur Wilmot, though maybe not so for Harold Morris, but to Arthur it felt necessary to quell the increasing doubts that seemed to be mounting in him the nearer the day of destiny approached.

And the irony was that as soon as he stepped over the threshold of 17 Oakshott Road he found himself totally engulfed once more into the turmoil of the arrangements and yet always with the sensation that he was merely an outsider looking in. It really was all getting too much for this reflective, insular man approaching middle life and trying desperately not to be swept along into this other world that was completely alien to what he knew or understood.

Even when the day finally arrived it was, as far as Arthur was concerned just a haze of being hustled here and pushed there, midst muffled sniggers at the height difference between the bride and groom and even to the fact of not actually being able to recall ever repeating any vows. The excuse for a reception in the small side function room of the King Charles Hotel was nothing less than farcical with the loudmouthed Mrs Ansell dominating the occasion with her demands and complaints about her requirements not being complied with. As a consequence the whole thing was over before it had even started, with the few guests disappearing into the public bar.

However, when it was all over and Arthur was confronted by the fact that he was now a married man, he also found himself sitting in his own room staring blankly at the night sky, the welcome night sky beyond his window. It had all been a frenetic mess as far as he was concerned and had culminated in Beatrice and Mrs Ansell retiring to their own rooms, using the excuse that it was because of tiredness and the stresses of the day.

The one fortunate outcome for Arthur, had been the decision that there was to be no honeymoon and for that fact alone Arthur was now very grateful and strangely it was with this thought and also with a resounding sense of relief that he laid his weary and confused head on his pillow. However, now that it was all over, now that the runaway train of the last few months had finally come to a grinding and pulverizing halt, his mind was now free to begin to delve into the awful and undeniable truths that his honour bound conscience had not allowed him to even consider before, thoughts that brought miniscule beads of sweat to his brow and which left him breathing uneasily within his dilemma.

For now in the darkness of his room with the moon's mocking face peering through his window, the truth of his situation became glaringly clear to him. And the truth was that this marriage was never going to work for all the reasons that his previous doubts and trepidations over long, uninterrupted periods of deep meditation on the bench outside the Refreshment Rooms on Platform 7 and the graveside of his sister Charlotte, had tried so hard to point out to him. And if he needed to isolate one compelling reason why it should not work, it was simply that, this marriage was a marriage of three people ...himself... Beatrice...and... Mrs Ansell!

He was also coming to terms with the fact that the two people who had signed the register were not what marriage was all about, being dependent in their own way on certain things that did not lend themselves to being part of a union. For he was a self reliant, independent man who preferred to place his tracks firmly down without any deviations in the landscape and Beatrice had been so long under her mother's domineering influence, that even if she had actually wanted to break away she could never have done so. And with these conclusions dancing inside his exhausted mind he finally gave in to sleep, a sleep that for the first time in many months was so deep that it was mercifully devoid of so many of the agitating problems needing a solution.

Arthur rose extra early next morning with the sole intention of seeking consolation with his weekly Sunday visit to Hockley Cemetery. And during the hour that he spent at Charlotte's graveside he was able to unburden himself of every aspect of the last few months in clear and concise detail. He was also able to admit just how foolish he had been in allowing his so well protected inner self to be opened up for scrutiny and then to be systematically drawn into the conniving machinations of his landlady, or should he now refer to her as his mother in law. And it was this abrupt realisation of their new association with each other that made him groan audibly.

And so, it was a very pensive and self absorbed Arthur who spent the rest of the day on the bench outside the Refreshment Rooms of Platform 7 on Snow Hill Station and yet completely oblivious to all the normal activity around him. Even as the trauma of the previous day's events began to subside in his mind, what was now replacing it were the full details of the absurd reality of his situation and these thoughts seemed to take precedence over everything else. But it was with an inkling of a wry smile when he finally concluded, that even though he was a married man with all the incumbent responsibilities that went with that status, he was seemingly somehow alone again, yes alone and it looked like that was what the future had now laid out for him after all.

And if Arthur had required his situation to be verified, it was when he dutifully presented himself at the rear parlour door of 17 Oakshott Road in anticipation of his Sunday tea. For the door was closed and so were the kitchen and the front sitting room doors. He even tried knocking and calling at each one but received no answer.

Nevertheless it was a somewhat relieved and rather thankful Arthur who finally climbed the stairs to his room and as he sat on the end of his bed gazing sightlessly out into the early evening dusk light, his thoughts took on a rather philosophical turn. For at no point he mused, had the simple endearing word 'love' ever passed between himself and Beatrice, not even the simple act of sharing a sealing kiss of intent. Even when he finally remembered to dutifully reciting the vows at the ceremony, he was also able to bring to mind how their true significance had completely passed him by in the delirium of the moment.

So what had he been thinking of these last few months and why had he permitted it to go as far as marriage, for there was nothing that even resembled the merest connection between himself and Beatrice, nothing that anyone could identify in them as even being a couple. And with these thoughts bursting like fireworks in his head the realisation suddenly hit him that he had been nothing less than one almighty, gullible fool to think that any form of love had ever existed in the first place.

Although it was never difficult for Arthur to interpret what love had come to mean to him, for he found it so easy to recall that sense of complete oneness his father and mother had shared with each other and it was also there in his own constant devotion to his sister Charlotte, even after all these years of her passing and nothing Arthur thought, could ever eclipse that. It was even possible for him to place into the equation the abiding sense of overwhelming serenity and calm he always seemed to find on the bench outside the Refreshment Rooms on Snow Hill Station. But for Arthur this was the full extent of his experiences in what he naively considered as being matters in any way associated with the heart.

It was then, as he continued to soak up the so familiar panorama through the window that he suddenly came to the crunching conclusion that it had been nothing less than blatant flattery mixed with the cloying attention shown to him by his landlady and her daughter that had guided him blindly to this fateful impasse. And although he was somehow able to formulate a mental impression for himself of what love between a man and a woman should be, with it having commitment, empathy and loyalty as fundamental ingredients, he was more than ever convinced that it was certainly not what existed between himself and Beatrice....his wife!

And as he continued to gaze out through the window at the evening dusk light he finally succumbed to sleep, a comforting kind of sleep that confirmed in his bewildered mind that he was once more where he always wanted to be.....Alone!

viii.
The Fly Trap

So the day's melted into weeks and then into months with the whole situation at Oakshott Road very speedily slipping back to where it had been before the fiasco of the wedding, or even the fateful birthday celebration of Beatrice for that matter. And yet, to all intents and purposes a marriage that had not been consummated by unspoken, yet seemingly mutual consent was really not a marriage and merely epitomised the gulf that had existed between Arthur and Beatrice from the very beginning. But to Arthur and his ingrained sense of honour, he was now married and whatever form that it took it was still a marriage. For it was his mother who had laid it out in her simple Methodist, Sunday School teachers moral code so many years before, that 'a promise made was a promise to be kept.'

Without any difficulty Arthur slotted back into his more than acceptable routine and he suspected his wife would be just as content in hers. He had his room and his privacy, he had his job and the bench on Platform 7 and that really was all he needed. The only difference now was the fact that he found himself not as a lodger paying forty two shillings a week but as a family provider, whereby he was now responsible for all the household bills.

However, as time went by it was the increasing demands that were being made on Arthur that convinced him more and more that he had somehow become a pawn in the unscrupulous scheming of the devious and despicable Mrs Ansell and even Beatrice. And even though he had accepted that the marriage had been nothing less than a complete charade, he had failed to realise the long term ramifications that were now being imposed on him. At last he was coming to terms of seeing himself as the biggest 'damned' fool that had ever walked god's earth and the consequences of his folly would boil over into his heavy ponderings as he sat on the bench outside the Refreshment Rooms on Platform 7. Even his silent conversations with his sister Charlotte at her graveside were taking on a much darker edge to them, with the anguish that was appearing in his words.

But it was the growing hurt inside this inwardly proud, honourable, yet quiet and inoffensive man that was of concern, for it was now maturing into emotions of hostility and contempt that seemed to be creeping into the remotest reaches of his inner soul. And with it were the danger signs of it fermenting into something far more all consuming. For nothing could diminish the sensation in Arthur, of him merely being caught like a fly in the shameless and deceitful trap of two vile and malicious minded women.

It was while he was in one such moment of cold, pensive scrutiny of his worsening situation that he allowed his mind a rare opportunity to delve into the past, only to find himself in the house in Digbeth with his parents and his sister Charlotte. Where during the summer months his father would place an empty jam jar on the window sill of the kitchen, but still with a very sticky inside and an inch or so of warm water in the bottom, as a ploy to tempt and entice any nuisance fly or wasp to enter. And Arthur would sit in a frozen fascination as the unsuspecting insects would enter the jar to either struggle in vain on the tacky sides or plummet into the goo in the bottom, either way his father's name for this simple device was very appropriate, it being the fly's 'suicide trap.'

And yet some did manage to free themselves from that ignominious demise, but the comparison with his own situation was so strong in Arthur's mind that he found himself muttering softly under his breath.....

"So must I!......So must I!.................So..... must.....I!."

A moment of infinite nostalgia on one hand, but a definitive moment of insight on the other and yet it was a moment and a conclusion that would stay well and truly lodged within him, like some annoying irritation that he desperately needed to scratch.

Be that as it may, events were to help reshape Arthur's waning morale when a mere four months after the sham wedding, Mr Soames required him to step into his office. It was there that he announced that Soames Footwear was expanding with the opening of three more shops, one each in Coventry, Bromsgrove and Wolverhampton. He also declared that Arthur was to be promoted to the position of 'Regional Manager' of all three new shops as well as the New Street branch. This would mean he had full responsibility of supervising, amongst all the other responsibilities of his new position, the staffing, layout of the floor space, purchasing, stock control and the actual opening of each new shop in turn. After that, Arthur would have under managers in each branch, answerable only to him, thus allowing him to retain full control over every aspect of the day to day running of all four branches. Mr Soames actually confided in Arthur that he had full confidence in him and he would be giving him complete authority in his decisions for making it a success. Arthur, in his usual humble manner had thanked him and said he would not let his employers trust be misplaced.

Of course all his expenses would be covered and there would be a substantial increase in his pay. He was also given the option of the use of a car and even though Arthur had learnt to drive during the war, albeit mainly in ambulances he declined, saying he preferred to use the railway. For Arthur this was indeed a great boost to his flagging spirits with the one significant bonus to this resounding good fortune in that he would now be able to travel on his beloved trains from his beloved Snow Hill Station. He was now a legitimate commuter with a real purpose for being on Platform 7 and with a destination to finally arrive at, travelling to each of the new shops at least one day a week.

And although Arthur saw himself as a married man with all the obligatory duties that went with that situation, he could not hide the overwhelming sense of freedom that his soul had been craving for and that Mr Soames' offer would now give him. For the atmosphere at 17 Oakshott Road was becoming very oppressive with Mrs Ansell making more and more demands on her new son in law, even though he was only considered to fit into that category in name only, having in reality returned to his previous status of lodger.

She had even taken to either ambush him as he came in or went out and had even presumed on numerous occasions to rap on his door late in the evening with curt demands for money for this or that. But it was the larger purchases that were the most daunting to Arthur, the new suite of furniture for the front sitting room, the new dressing table for his wife's room, the new carpet for the landing and stairs, the installation of gas fires into both Mrs Ansell and Beatrice's bed rooms and the list went on and on and well beyond the everyday needs of the household. And all the pleasantness and smiles that had been so much a part of the facade before that fateful day of the wedding, when he had been mindlessly drawn into the presence of the registrar to stand next to Beatrice, had now disappeared completely.

Arthur had become a victim of his own good but malleable nature, which was now depriving him of the ability to even argue against any of the demands that were being made on him. More and more with the sense of betrayal biting deep into that hidden sensitivity, Arthur began to despise his whole situation. So often now in his more reflective moods he found himself damning his stupidity and weakness of character in allowing himself to be so easily manoeuvred into a marriage, merely as a form of support for Beatrice and her mother. He rightly concluded that he had been so blind to have been duped into this matrimonial mockery without ever stopping to fully consider all the connotations that would accompany it. More and more nothing could diminish the overwhelming sensation of merely being caught like a fly in the 'suicide trap' by two unscrupulous women.

But now in hindsight he also realised that he would not have had the forcefulness in his character to have found a way out. He was not a bitter man by nature, with a simple philosophy that implied that all he wanted was to be allowed to live his life in his own way without interference. In return he would never impose himself or his ideals on anyone else. And this belief had seen him through six years of war time service earning great respect from all who had worked with him. But now all that was being trampled underfoot and yet typically, he was blaming himself for being so easily cornered and exploited. And yet he did feel that he could now justify his somewhat devious act of taking the bulk of his savings out of his Lloyds Bank account and placing it into a Barclays Bank under the pseudonym of Harold Morris.

In spite of all that, on one particular evening, a week or so after Mr Soames' offer had been made Arthur, out of a strange mix of courtesy and duty knocked lightly on the door of the front sitting room of his lodgings. And even though he could hear muttered voices and the shuffling of feet it took more than three minutes before the door was brusquely thrown open.

"What do yer want!" was the terse greeting he received from the ever smoking Mrs Ansell.

Arthur then briefly explained some of the details of the changes to his employment at Soames Footwear but with no reference to it being a promotion, merely highlighting the fact that it would incur irregular hours due to his travelling from branch to branch.

Mrs Ansell stood thoughtfully poised in the doorway for a few moments, pulling heavily on her Woodbine before making any reply.

"Well!" she drawled, while stretching herself to her full three inch height difference over her son in law, merely in an attempt to intimidate him. "I hope that means.... there'll be more money!"

Then, to conclude the matter, she deliberately aimed a cloud of acrid tobacco smoke into Arthur's eyes, forcing him to step back with the smarting pain that it caused him, while his stunned mind attempted to cope with the amount of contemptuous bile that had been contained in those few words and delivered with so much smug satisfaction. But the culminating indignity came when the door was then forcibly slammed shut, to be followed by a chorus of stifled sniggering from the other side.

With the sound of the scornful sniggering still ringing in his ears, Arthur turned and made his way heavily along the hallway and up the stairs, as the cold, demanding harshness of Mrs Ansell's words throbbed incessantly between his temples. Even when he stopped to peer over the banister into the void of the stair well and the hallway below, his head was again filled with the crushing humiliation that he had felt as the front sitting room door was callously slammed in his face.

For many a minute he just stood and stared down into the stair well that seemed like the dark abyss of his soul, as the glowing truth of what this all meant began to illuminate through the blinkered acceptance of his naive, trusting nature. Nothing he thought, but a prize, witless idiot could have succumbed to the flattering, wily attentions of these two such devious women, who had only been interested in trapping him for their own grasping gains. And the sad glaring truth, which was now bellowing loudly inside his head.....was that he....Arthur Wilmot..... was that prize, witless idiot. And while he was digesting this glaring admission the comparison of him being the fly that had been caught in the 'suicide trap' once again took precedence in his thoughts.

Even so, it was now becoming crystal clear to this normally quiet, mild mannered man that this one final degrading episode simply encompassed the whole wretched situation he had allowed himself to fall into. At last he was able to discard the restricting blinkered vision and truly see for the first time the cold-hearted, deceptive cunning of Mrs Ansell and her daughter.

And it was much later still, as he stood glaring out of his window at the clear night sky beyond, that he really sensed that the final nail in the coffin of his existence at Oakshott Road was being hammered home with a vengeance. For it was one sentence of five seemingly innocuous words that were now resonating loudly in his head as if to confirm this damning conclusion.

'Until death do you part!'

Nevertheless, by way of gaining some kind of comfort to the damaged integrity of his soul, he reached into the wardrobe and once more placed the contents of his father's leather tool bag onto his bed. Slowly he fingered and touched each item in turn, the Hornby Train Set, the wooden engine and the Boys Own Annuals and cigarette cards. And gradually, with the soothing thoughts that accompanied the familiar feel they gave him, he was able to ease the torment that had been simmering inside him like a boiler just ready to explode.

Still very thoughtful but much calmer, he then took his wallet from his inside pocket and gently drew out the small leather envelope containing his sister's lock of auburn hair that could glint with strands of gold in the sunlight and carefully pushing his fore finger inside, he was able, once again to feel the softness of each strand. And instantly the sense of tranquillity and well being he always experienced washed over him and for the millionth time he could almost visualise her there with him in his little room. It was always such a comforting sensation for him when his world seemed to be turned upside down with no answers to be found anywhere else.

For he was now fully aware of not only the extent of Mrs Ansell and Beatrice's scheming and plotting but also the depth of his own supreme folly and sheer degradation. This proud man, who had merely been seeking companionship from his marriage, had been cruelly and selfishly used by the two women and it was now very clear to him that they expected that situation to continue. It now stood out like a beacon to Arthur, that even though he had nurtured feelings for Beatrice, the simple fact was that she had been totally complicit in the deception and now trusted to his honourable nature to stand by the promises he had made to her, as his wife.

'Until death do you part!'

But to Arthur the growing distaste for these two women was turning into downright enmity for everything they had done to him and everything that they were still capable of doing and the outcome was that he now had to cope with emotions that he had never experienced before. And it was not a pleasant realisation that this poisonous mixture was developing into a seething sensation of repulsion for his landlady and her daughter, for he could no longer refer to them as his mother in law or even his wife.

What had he become, nothing less than a replacement for the late Mr Ansell as a provider and a willing victim of the bullying tactics of a manipulating witch and her black cat. It was true there had been no real physical harassment or derisory remarks, at least not in his hearing, as it had been so many years before in his youth. For now the bullying was far more subtle and effective and aimed purely at that vulnerable side to his nature, his integrity, his honour and most all his loneliness. And with this blatant admission of his frailties eating away inside his head, his eyes became glazed over with the shame of it, the shame of realising just how much his good nature and his good intentions had been so cruelly used and thrown back in his face.

Once again he allowed his attention to be taken by the night sky above the roof tops as he wistfully peered through the window, while striving to fill his mind with absolute nothingness. And yet, even as he maintained his somewhat mesmerized gaze a number of strangely faint pale blurs began to appear on the glass window panes, causing Arthur to peer even harder with increasing curiosity.

At first the blurs were so indistinct that Arthur struggled to see if they were marks on the glass or smudges on the outside, or even something being reflected from inside the room and onto the dark windowpanes. But then, one by one the faint blurs seemed to take shape, so that as they gained definition he was able to clearly identify them as being faces, the faces of the antagonists from his youth so many years ago. The faces of those who had sought to derive so much sadistic satisfaction at his expense and who had chased and pushed and called out names and cutting remarks at every opportunity, with Charlotte his sister, constantly intervening to the detriment of her own safety on many occasions. Even now, as he stood transfixed by what his eyes were telling him, he could hear again the tirade of humiliating insults, pummelling inside his head, that had filled those early years of his youth and he could even see framed in the glass of the window the pitiless expressions of triumph, as the arrows of abuse struck home with a vengeance.

And midst the evil, smirking faces another face was emerging on the framed glass of the window and it was a face full of malicious, bullish spite. A face that Arthur instantly recognised and one that even as he stared into its eyes was producing so much loathing to flow within him that he had to physically shake himself free of the strange and distressing sensation it was causing. And yet the more he stared the more the feeling of hatred was creeping into him to upset him even more. For the face that was now sneering so contemptuously back from the window was in fact the face of his landlady......Mrs Clarissa Mary Ansell.

Then seeping through those almost witchlike features was another face, pale and hauntingly gaunt but with such an evil glint in the eyes that it caused Arthur to reel back as a cold shiver ran up and down his spine. It was then that both faces, that of Mrs Ansell and her daughter Beatrice melted into one shimmering fusion that glared out at Arthur with mocking, scornful expressions. And for a long agonizing moment the apparitions soundlessly taunted him before gradually fading from view to leave Arthur with his heart beating like a steam hammer and his breath coming in short, sharp gasps, but thankfully, once more with the welcome night sky above the rooftops framed in the glass of his window.

Feverishly rubbing his eyes Arthur sank down heavily onto his bed and attempted to rationalize exactly what had just occurred. But his head was so full of contradictions and questions that finally his ingrained stoicism forced its way through to gradually erase from his mind all the fearful anguish that the disturbing images and memories the gang of tormentors from his youth, along with those of his landlady and her daughter had cruelly left him with. And as his breathing and heart beats began to come under control, he was then able to logically discount the brief but troubling apparitions as nothing more than figments of his disturbed state of mind, compounded by the stresses of his situation and his recent humiliating encounter with his land lady.

But all of this was now leaving a very bad, bitter taste in Arthur's mouth, the bitter taste of uncompromising retribution which he was finding very hard indeed to reconcile himself to. For Arthur was not a spiteful or vengeful person by nature, but something dire was now corrupting his normally placid disposition and igniting a fire inside him, a burning sensation that was demanding that he must regain his lost, fragile self esteem. That he must seek a suitable, permanent redress on those that had defiled and debased his sincere sense of honour. Strong words indeed for this normally quiet, unassuming man to even think, let alone consider as a form of action. And they were words that would continue to smoulder deep into his psyche long after this moment when he had first brought them to mind.

Equally, for Arthur to come to terms with so much change in his perspective of himself and to admit to the growing need for revenge was as if the ostrich in his character had finally pulled its head out of the sand and was seeking the light of undeniable reasoning for the very first time. But with that light came a strange awareness, that of feeling more lonely and vulnerable than at any other point in his life and the emptiness that it brought with it materialised into such a deep felt sigh of forlorn hope. And yet, ironically even as he sighed this plaintive sigh of despair, the sigh slowly transformed into a sigh of contended justification, as an uncharacteristic glimmer for a recipe of vengeful just deserts, began to formulate in his mind.

ix.
The Leather Tool Bag

Arthur was able to drop into his new life as Regional Manager with Soames Footwear's new shops with an enthusiasm that even Mr Isaac Soames quietly applauded. The ideas and decisions flowed from Arthur and with the opening of the first of the shops in the centre of Coventry in Coronation week of 1953, it was clear to all that it was going to be a success. But it was not so much the opening of the shop that gave Arthur so much pleasure and quiet gratification, it was the fact that he could now use his new position to spend as little time as possible at 17 Oakshott Road.

Even so this did not seem to perturb Mrs Ansell or her infrequently seen daughter, who were only concerned that there life style was not interfered with in any way. In the whole of the time since the wedding Arthur had only clapped his eyes on Beatrice on half a dozen occasions and each time she had deliberately avoided any contact with him, either by eye or by word. Although Arthur was not at all distressed by this, for he had now accepted exactly where his place was and that was merely as a lodger and honour bound provider.

However the Sunday vigils at the graveside of his sister Charlotte had continued to yield some comfort to the tortured sensitivity of this quiet, unassuming man. More and more Arthur had unburdened himself of all his troubles in a suppressed yet desperate outpouring of emotion in the hope that he would hear the silent words of his sister, speaking to him within his inner listening ear. Words to console his agonised soul and words to ease all the flagrant torments of what he had come to consider as his foolishly self inflicted status at Oakshott Road.

With his eyes shut tight and with his hands trembling, he would clutch the leather envelope that contained the lock of auburn hair. And the depth of his anxieties would manifest themselves in a chill shudder throughout his diminutive frame, while swaying gently from side to side in the devout hope that one day his prayers would be answered and he would not only hear her soft voice speaking within him but his eyes would open to find her there, not in his imagination, but there before him just one more time. And as Sunday followed Sunday, with Arthur maintaining his attentive vigil at the graveside of his sister, never once was the urgency of his pleas ever lessened through disappointment as each week passed.

But there was a ponderous dark reality to the days for Arthur. And it became such a heartfelt yearning within him, for his ardent prayers to be answered, that on one particular Sunday, the Sunday following the opening of the Coventry branch of Soames Footwear, that was to be the one Sunday so different to every other Sunday and so very, very special. Because when Arthur, with his eyes closed tightly in silent prayer called out with his passionate appeal for Charlotte to speak to him……to appear before him…..she did!

She answered by softly, yet clearly speaking his name and the nearness of her voice encouraged him to slowly open his eyes and to look up. And it was with an incredulous expression and a sudden dryness in his throat that Arthur was able to focus on a figure that was no more than a yard or so away. For there before him, standing beside her own grave was his sister, his beloved sister Charlotte with her auburn hair cascading over her shoulders as the morning sunlight picked out the golden strands.

In a constrained mix of awe and disbelief Arthur rubbed his eyes, for Charlotte was actually there in touching distance, so real and this time not locked away in his memory, in his imagination. Charlotte, in a flowery dress and with that familiar and welcoming smile that he had so often longed to see just once more and now she was there, standing before him and exactly how he always remembered her before the dreaded tuberculosis had begun to take a hold.

"Charlotte!" he breathed in exasperation. "Oh......Oh.....Char.. Charlotte!"

"Arthur.....dear Arthur!" the gentle voice whispered in reply.

Arthur stretched out a hand as his sister did the same and he could feel the softness of her touch on his fingers. For long moments they stood gazing at each other as if the years that had separated them since Charlotte's death had been no more than a miniscule glitch in time. Then without any movement of her lips Arthur could hear her tender tones speaking to him, surrounding him with so much warmth of emotion that he had never ever felt before.

"Arthur....my dear, dear Arthur," her voice softly sighed. "So many times you've stood where you now stand.....So many times you've heard my voice speaking.... within you.....without seeing me.... But each time dear Arthur...I have been with you...close to you...by your side.....Never fear my dear brother and know this....that I will be with you always."

Charlotte's voice paused for a moment as Arthur soaked up the sheer, unutterable magic of the moment. Then his sister continued with a slight tilt of her head as if to emphasise what she had to say.

"And yet.... I'm here now to say to you....that all your trials will only be resolved by the cleansing of all the hurt in your soul....For the evil that is being done to you my dear brother.... must be avenged!"

"Charlotte!" Arthur repeated, for his mind was so enraptured by the vision of his sister that any other words he wanted to say were lost to him.

"My time with you my dear brother..... is short......But heed what I say.....You must avenge the evil transgressions on the purity of your soul......dear...dear Arthur!

And with those words stirring a multitude of thoughts in his head Arthur watched in wonderment as the figure of his sister began to dissolve before his eyes.

"Please!...please don't go....don't leave me again!" Arthur begged as he moved towards the dwindling image of his sister. "Please....." he repeated earnestly. "Please!"

"I must.....dear Arthur!" was Charlotte's sad response. "But I will be waiting for you!"

And in a final misty, shimmering haze she was gone.

Arthur stood totally enthralled by what his eyes had been showing him and what his ears had heard. In all his weekly visits to this place that he had made over so many years, never before had his sister actually appeared to him. Yes, he had spoken to her and he had heard her voice speaking to him inside his head, while imagining that he could really see her and all the time never doubting that she was at least, somewhere close by watching over him. And yet, now it had been confirmed, in Charlotte's own words that she had always been there with him on every occasion, invisible to his eyes maybe but with him, watching and guiding him as she had always done when she was alive.

But this Sunday it was so profoundly significant to Arthur in that she had actually been there, standing before him, speaking to him, touching him and with it all so clear in his mind. She had spoken to him face to face, comforting him by saying she would always be with him. And for the first time since she had died he did not feel so alone, for he could still feel the warmth that her presence had given him as she stood before him by her own graveside.

It was then that the words she had spoken once again resonated in his mind, the words that amounted to nothing less than a warning, a warning that he must avenge himself on his tormentors so as to purge his soul of all the hurt that it had been subjected to. All of which would now become the catalyst that would dictate all that was to follow. And that was to mean for Arthur to put into place a scheme for vengeance, a scheme that, even as he stood gazing at the ground that his sister had so recently occupied, had been forming subliminally inside his head. Since in fact, the evening of his humiliation by the vile tongue of his land lady, an episode that even as it was happening Arthur had somehow realised was to have far reaching consequences and in reality just needing the final spur of his sister's words to move his formula for vengeance forward.

And so, to bring about his vengeful plan, his first move over the next few days was to become his alter ego Harold Morris, who had opened a savings account with Barclays Bank. This was achieved with a visit to a second hand shop in a side street near to Snow Hill Station to purchase a brown suit and brogue shoes, a rather well worn raincoat, shirts and ties, a trilby hat, horn rimmed spectacles and a leather suitcase. The final touch was the purchase of a crusty, well chewed old pipe as a distracting prop, even though Arthur was a confirmed non smoker. All this to transform him into what he believed a travelling salesman would look like and behave like, because Arthur saw Harold Morris in such a role.

To aid the metamorphosis he next visited a theatrical costumier in another side street where he selected a slightly bushy, greyish brown moustache and hair piece, mainly to add age to his outward appearance but also as a way of detracting attention from his own fair colouring. And even though he hoped he would never be subjected to a close inspection he was very careful to make sure that every detail looked as authentic to his proposed character as possible.

Then on the following Saturday he chose to arrange his visit to the newly opened Soames Footwear shop in the centre of Coventry. While he was there he took the opportunity of utilizing the Coventry stations toilets to change into the guise of Harold Morris and to take a dowdy little room in a back street near to the station for thirty five shillings a week and telling the aging landlady Mrs Petrie, that he would only need it for two or three days a week as a base when he was in the Coventry area. So paying two months in advance he was given a key and told that providing he was quiet he could come and go as he pleased.

From there it was back to Coventry Station, to change once more into Arthur and then onto Snow Hill Station to leave Harold in the suitcase he had purchased and then to deposit the suitcase in the left luggage office to await the time when Harold would be needed again. All in all, a very successful trial run of a fundamental part of his planning, Arthur considered somewhat thoughtfully, as he made his way out of the station through the glass domed, booking hall concourse.

Having said that, for some inexplicable reason on that early Saturday evening, a rather weary but somewhat satisfied Arthur decided to forgo his customary stopover on the bench outside the Refreshment Rooms on Platform 7 and take the earlier bus to speed him to the refuge of his room and his self imposed but welcome isolation.

On reaching his bus stop it was only a short, five minute walk from there to his lodgings, but as he turned the corner into the rather pleasant shade of the tree lined Oakshott Road, he gradually became aware of something that made him slow his pace to a point that it finally brought him to an abrupt, stunned halt. In fact it was necessary for him to correct his trembling body by grabbing at a convenient tree trunk for the support that it offered. For swinging on the gate of number 18 Oakshott Road, the adjoining semi to number 17 was a little girl in a flowery dress but with long auburn locks cascading over her shoulders, for all the world the image of his sister Charlotte at the age of ten or eleven.

Plunging his quivering hand into his trouser pocket he pulled out his handkerchief to dab away the small droplets of perspiration that had somehow gathered beneath his trilby hat and across his brow. Surely his eyes were deceiving him, surely what he was seeing was a ghost, a dream, some kind of hallucination, but surely it could not really be his sister. For many minutes Arthur stood totally absorbed and transfixed by what his eyes were trying to tell him but once the initial shock had subsided he was able to stand and fondly watch as an unstoppable torrent of nostalgia flooded through his mind. That was until the reality of the moment began to dawn on him and he was able to rationalise what it all seemed to mean.

For when his sister had appeared before him, standing by her own graveside just a few days earlier it had felt absolutely the most natural thing in the world. It was almost as if he had expected her to come to him sooner or later, simply because of his deep desire to see her, to talk to her and for her to talk to him. Now in his heart he was certain that Charlotte had always been looking over him, guiding him and even more certain now that she always would. But what he was seeing before him now was totally out of context to his reasoning, logical mind and yet what he was being confronted by looked so real, even though the little girl's actual face was obscured by the long auburn locks of hair.

Quickly scanning round to see if anyone had noticed his few minutes of uncertainty and confusion, he began to walk very slowly towards what he was now convinced was the living incarnation of his beloved sister, though dead now some thirty years. And as he got closer the little girl turned to face him, her rosy cheeks beaming a smile.

"Hello!" she chirped merrily Arthur did not answer straight away as he fiddled with the latch on the gate to his lodgings, though totally enthralled at the now astounding resemblance of this sparkling, auburn haired little girl to his sister Charlotte at the same age. In the end all he could manage was a shy smile as a response, before opening the gate and hurriedly striding towards the front door. And as he reached it he contrived to glance round briefly for a moment to be greeted once more by another winning smile.

Even so it was now a moment that seemed to last forever, for there was very little beauty in the sad, colourless world of Arthur Wilmot and so he allowed the moment to take his mind speedily back to the family lodgings in Digbeth, a lifetime ago. And as he did the years seemed to sweep by into infinity leaving him with the lustrous sensation of his sister's hair in his fingers as he carefully brushed it and always with her smile as a reflection in the dressing table mirror, the smile that had been for him and for him alone.

But now it was the quizzical expression that appeared on the face of the smiling little girl as she caught the small man staring at her that finally broke the moment into a million pieces for Arthur and forcing him clumsily through the door and into the house.

His first instinct when he reached his room was to instantly take the leather envelope containing the lock of his sister's hair from his wallet and for many minutes he sat on the bed with his mind drifting wistfully back with so many thoughts and images crowding in for his attention. So many that meant so much to this man who was only content dwelling in his own isolation, an isolation that he was now so grateful to have re-established. And even as his fingers touched those soft strands of auburn hair he knew instantly that his sister was there with him, beside him, even though on this occasion he could not actually see her.

Replacing the envelope with the lock of hair back into his wallet, he then went to the wardrobe to take out his father's leather tool bag with those other precious items from his past.

But it was not there!

Instantly his mind froze, for he had lost all of his ability to think, but then panic stepped in and he frantically tore round the small room, stripping his bed, emptying the wardrobe and the chest of drawers. He even lifted the bed away from the wall to search behind it and under it. Only after a breathless five minutes was he finally convinced that the tool bag was not in the room.

Arthur stood disbelieving what his instincts were telling him was the truth, that his precious tool bag could only have been removed by someone in the house. With his head swimming and with a growing sensation of nausea creeping over him he stood in perfect silence as he leant his throbbing head against the wardrobe door in a bewildering state of utter despair. Something began to bubble deep within him, a sensation that was totally foreign to him and one that he had not even experienced during his war service years. It was a sensation that he was finding very difficult to control as a blinding, uncharacteristic anger began to seethe within him, causing his clenched fist to drum against his temple in time to the rhythmic pounding of his heart, as the whites of his eyes suddenly began to glaze over in a gathering mist of red.

In a simmering daze Arthur very slowly, very purposefully opened the door of his room and made his way down the stairs to stand before the front sitting room door, all the time desperately trying to restrain the insatiable intensity of the fury that seemed to be consuming the whole of his normally rational and well balanced bearing.

Taking in a deep breath he rapped sharply on the door.

There was no answer.

He rapped harder.

Still there was no answer.

Now he adjusted the rapping to a furious heavy banging.

Instantly the door swung open and he was confronted by the stern, uncompromising countenance of Mrs Ansell, arms folded aggressively and the inevitable cigarette dangling from the corner of her mouth.

"What do yer want?" she rasped indignantly through a cloud of blue smoke.

Arthur looked her straight in the eye and quenching the need to exhibit the thriving rage within him, he politely requested to be told the whereabouts of his possessions.

"The church had a jumble sale today," Mrs Ansell announced with an air of smug satisfaction in her voice. "That's where your toys have gone!..... Anyway!" she sniggered. "What's a man...even one your size, be doing playing with toys!"

And with that the door was slammed heavily in his face.

x.
Man On A Mission

Arthur did not go back to his room he just stood for a few moments in a state of fuming outrage, before turning abruptly and walking straight out of the front door of 17 Oakshott Road to catch the bus into Birmingham and to seek refuge in the one place that his soul could find the peace that it now sorely craved. And there on the bench outside the Refreshment Rooms on Platform 7 he sat oblivious of time and equally oblivious of all the fleeting shadows that passed before him.

In a kind of traumatised stupor he attempted to come to terms with what had happened and to try and rationalise his landlady's devilish actions. However, the only conclusion he could come to was that he was now totally committed to the course of retribution that he had been deliberating over since the Sunday of his sister's warning.

For a long while his mind dwelt heavily on the loss of the tool bag and its contents, all of which were irreplaceable in the extreme. The fact was that not only were those items precious to him in their own right but so were the memories that were deeply instilled in their fabric. And even though this humble and modest man had never written to claim his rightful campaign and service medals when he had been demobbed after the war, his one last material memory of his wartime service had also gone, that being the letter of commendation from his commanding officer which had been between the pages of one of the albums.

But now this final penetrating humiliation on the part of Mrs Ansell was, to put it quite simply, the last straw, the final concluding action that sealed the fate of this totally evil and heartless woman and her equally complicit daughter and all their treacherous manipulations. And Arthur was viewing it exactly in that light, as a complete betrayal of his trust and his honesty and he was now fully resigned on the inevitability of the bitter, deadly path he was to take.

Even so, as he sat thoughtfully mulling over the route that had brought him to this point, so much seemed to crowd his mind for consideration. His thinking began to question why he had decided, so early on, to have his mail redirected to the newsagents accommodation address and then to the reasoning behind his deliberate act of changing his Lloyds bank account to a Barclays Bank savings account, which in turn required the devious but necessary creation of the name Harold Morris. Was this all purely a simple stratagem for self preservation, or an intuitive insight into what was to come. There were so many why's and wherefore's erupting now in Arthur's head that he had to consciously focus his thinking on the present and to give it his full attention.

And as the platform clock steadily ate up the minutes, with the trains and the people going about their business unnoticed by the totally preoccupied Arthur, the furrows on the brow of this slight of stature figure began to deepen with the gravity of where his thinking was taking him. For now that he had decided on one particular path to follow, the determination that was an inherent quality in Arthur was not going to allow him to be diverted from it. And it was all being thought through with such a cold sense of purpose, that if Arthur had been a bystander looking down on himself then he would have been truly shocked at the thought patterns his mind was undertaking. For the cloud of utter humiliation and shame that he was suffering under was cutting out any glimpses of reason or conscience, leaving nothing but the corrupting canker of revenge to eat into him. And if that was to be the direction he must take to cleanse all the hurt and pain in his soul, then anything less would not be enough for Arthur Wilmot.

But true revenge needs to be planned for and not hurried. It needs not to come out of anger because that only masks the sense of satisfaction. It also needs a subtlety to it that leaves no trace of the avenger in its wake for the authorities to pick up on. And yet this normally quiet and retiring man was now pondering heavily on every aspect of what he wanted from the vengeful scheme that was forming in his mind.

And as the platform clock indicated midnight, Arthur once again reached inside his wallet and drew out the little leather envelope containing the lock of his sister's hair and he breathed a sigh of relief. The sigh was not purely for the fact that he was grateful it had not been in his leather tool bag to end up as a source of even more ridicule at the hands of his landlady and her daughter, but the sigh was also a sigh of resolve for the fact that now his mind was firmly set on what he must do.

With the clock hands moving from the midnight position he suddenly realised it was now Sunday morning but nothing induced him to move and so he remained deeply immersed in his thoughts. Occasionally a member of the railway night staff would pass by and give him a curious look and even a railway police officer approached to ask if he was alright. But everyone knew the man who seemed to spend so much time on the bench outside the Refreshment Rooms on Platform 7 and so they were not unduly concerned.

It was not until the first of the passengers began to congregate on the platform for the early trains and the buzz of activity emanated from the staff in the Refreshment Rooms that Arthur finally made to move. Very stiffly with the morning chill in his bones he made his way along the platform to the flight of steps that led to the bridge and the main concourse. But the Arthur that had risen from that bench was a very different Arthur that had sat down on it over nine hours before. For this Arthur now had a definite motivation and plan lodged in his head and he was determined he would see it through to its inevitable, bitter conclusion.

It was later still that he stood looking down on the grave of his beloved sister, with the leather envelope containing the strands of her auburn hair in his hand and seeking her silent approval of his scheme. There, with the morning dew still beneath his feet, he thought his thoughts in such a profound manner, swaying slightly from side to side in the sheer rapture of the moment, while listening and concentrating carefully until he could hear the cherished voice of his sister Charlotte speaking to him so clearly inside his head. And the words he could hear were the words of his sister's approval and which now confirmed to Arthur that the path of vengeance he had chosen to walk down was the right and correct path to follow.

And even as he stood there, with his eyes closed in sublime unity with his beloved sister, he could once again visualize quite clearly her sweet, well defined features, smiling that vibrant, welcoming smile that seared deep into his mind, as it always did when each time he stood in this place.

But then, something else was materialising, for gradually the features of his sister appeared to filter into those of the little girl from number 18, smiling the same smile that had etched itself so deep into his memory the instant that it had enchanted him the night before. The smile that even now was bringing something of a secret, upward creasing on Arthur's own lips and a softening of his usually austere countenance. And his heart seemed to beat that little bit faster as the mental picture that his mind was presenting to him only seemed to emphasise the astonishing resemblance between the little girl and his sister at the same age. So much so that even though Arthur's breathing was coming in short, breathless gasps of subdued exhilaration, he refrained from opening his eyes for fear of losing the delicate image that lay embedded behind his lids.

Sadly though, the moment was all too brief for him and within just a few tantalising seconds the image had mistily evaporated away to find residency in some subconscious recess of his memory.

It took many minutes for him to compose himself and to overcome the shivering in his limbs and the chill that had set in throughout the whole of his slight body. And yet as he began to walk away from his sisters graveside there was now a lightness in the step of Arthur Wilmot, a lightness that he realised he must control to maintain a semblance of normality about his general demeanour. For there was also a deep seated realisation within him that he was now a man with a definite purpose, he was a man on a mission to be completed with all the innate emotional indifference that he knew he was certainly capable of.

It is a cruel fact, that when the creeping curse of obsession takes over the whole of your focus and dominates every waking moment, then nothing else seems to matter, nothing else has any true relevance in your life. Very much like walking down a long dark tunnel with your periphery vision so impaired that no light can infiltrate and divert you from that which is upper most in your mind. And upper most in Arthur's mind, with its brooding sense of purpose, was to avenge the deep, deep cavern of inconsolable hurt which had now been compounded by the loss of his precious leather tool bag and its contents.

And yet, in reality there was not a bad bone in Arthur's body. From an early age he had suffered greatly from the bullying and verbal abuse that had been so freely dished out by the louts at his school and that had tended to harden him against societies lack of tolerance of something slightly different from the accepted norm. For whatever respect that Arthur had been awarded to him over the years had been fiercely won, even when in the service of his country all those around him had come to accept and appreciate the little man's qualities and strengths.

But nothing had prepared his so well hidden sensitivity of nature from the calculated and contrived programme of humiliation and indignity that was being poured on him by his landlady and her daughter. They had carried him to the heights that his emotional limit would allow by showing him a warmth of companionship that he had not experienced since he was very young. And all for the purpose of ensnaring him, simply for their own mercenary ends by thinking that with his marriage to Beatrice he would be totally honour bound and malleable to their controlling ways.

Nevertheless enough was enough, for not only was Arthur the target of their sheer vindictive and sadistic ways but they were bleeding him dry with their constant demands for money. And now the generous wages from Soames Footwear was not even coping with those demands, for he was beginning to eat into the one hundred pounds that he had deliberately left in his account at Lloyds Bank.

He had considered a number of escape plans, including the totally unacceptable route of divorce, which contradicted all of his principles, for in his eyes his own well established moral code demanded that he respected and kept his marriage vows and nothing could sway him from that. There was also the option of just walking out one morning and never to return. But even that route seemed unacceptable to Arthur, for his steadfast attitude in all things demanded some kind of defining resolution to the problem, some kind of complete closure. And equally he was under no illusion to think that neither, Mrs Ansell or Beatrice would ever allow their 'golden goose' to lay eggs anywhere other than at their door.

Arthur had come to the conclusion of truly believing that they would do everything in their power to prevent him from even thinking he could leave, let alone divorce Beatrice and so he would never be free of the purgatory that they continually dished out on a daily basis. It was also a fact that he had now come to resent every last farthing that they manipulated from him, so he was not going to put himself into a position whereby through divorce his honourable nature would demand that he would continue to provide for them.

No, he was totally convinced that he must bow his head to the devil and accept that there was but one permanent solution open to him. A permanent solution that would both rid himself of the grinding responsibilities imposed on him through his sham marriage to Beatrice and a permanent solution without any repercussions on him in the future. Merely to cut off the offending cankered branch to clear the tree to mature unaffected.

And so it was that Arthur Wilmot had put his well thought out plan into operation with the activation of Harold Morris, which allowed him to slip easily between the two worlds of Oakshott Road and the travelling salesman in Coventry. For as Arthur he arranged to dutifully return to his lodgings perhaps three or four nights a week, simply to keep a kind of continuity to his movements for the benefit of Mrs Ansell.

The other nights, Arthur retrieved his case which contained his travelling salesman disguise from the left luggage office on Snow Hill Station. Then after changing in the gents toilet he reappeared as Harold Morris who then travelled by train to Coventry Station. From there, it was as Harold Morris the travelling salesman with his case of imaginary wares who bought his supper at the fish and chip shop on the corner of the street to his lodgings and who then spent the night in the rather seedy room he was renting. The whole purpose being to establish a recognisable character for the locals, that he might need to permanently assume at a later date.

Next morning the process was reversed with Harold Morris leaving his lodgings for the short walk to the station where he boarded a train to Snow Hill. There he entered the gents toilet as Harold Morris and reappeared as Arthur Wilmot, once more depositing his case at the left luggage before pursuing his Regional Manager's responsibilities with Soames Footwear.

And when the time came to put the final part of his vengeful plan into action he would be able to either ride out the storm of a possible inquest as Arthur Wilmot, or disappear completely and emerge like a butterfly as Harold Morris.

However, he also realised that he would have regrets, one being the happy situation he had in Mr Soames employ. But when he delved into the full picture of his life as it was now, he could do nothing but come to the conclusion that if is well thought out stratagem was to go awry, then leaving his so satisfying job would in fact be a very small sacrifice to make.

Even so, as the weeks went by there was one small issue that was slightly marring the plans that Arthur was making, one minor blip in the full scheme of things that had risen to infiltrate through the iron guard to his emotions and to at least provide him with a sense of diversion from the intensity of his revenge filled thoughts. Equally it was a minor blip that seemed to bring a certain consolation to him and one that, whenever possible he would seek out by timing his arrival down the road to his lodgings to coincide with the after tea hour when the little girl with long auburn locks would be in the front garden of number 18 Oakshott Road.

Arthur quite often slowed his pace or even stopped to just nostalgically watch her, either playing some imaginary game for one, or skipping with her rope, or more often than not just harmlessly amusing herself by swinging gently backwards and forwards on the gate. And yet, he could not get it out of his mind the compelling resemblance this auburn haired little girl had with his sister, for to Arthur she was nothing less than the living embodiment of every memory he possessed of Charlotte at that age. From the lustrous nature of her long auburn tresses, that like his sister even glinted with gold strands in the sunlight, to the sensitive sparkle in her hazel eyes. Even to the open, welcoming smile, which was always there with a cheery greeting to anyone who passed her gate and it seemed that there was always a special one for Arthur, who had now managed to quell his innate shyness to respond with his own smile and cheery wave for little Amy Morton. For that was the little girl's name.

And even though there were so many conflicting thoughts that seemed to occupy Arthur's head on a daily basis, there was that certain thankful joy he derived from every fleeting glimpse of little Amy Morton. And many a time now, his mind's eye would play tricks on him by conjuring up an image of both Amy's face and Charlotte's face melting and moving like overlaying photograph negatives and resulting into one perfectly developed picture, so profoundly close was the similarity between the two, so indivisible were each with each other.

So the days and weeks passed by, and this deepening impression took on a kind of unity between the two images and became ever more unsettling for Arthur, to such an extent that he began to see them as a singular entity, as one person at two stages in one life. One bright light in an otherwise very dark sky that now seemed to surround his very existence.

It was quite by accident that Arthur had been able to learn that the little girl's name was Amy Morton and that she had moved into two of the rooms of number 18 Oakshott Road with her mother. Arthur had managed to glean this information through Mrs Stevens at the local post office, who had the reputation of being the font of all the gossip in the area, when she had been discussing the 'new people' with another customer.

Arthur had also learnt that Amy's mother was a widow after losing her husband, a pilot who had been killed in July 1948 during the Berlin Airlift. It also transpired that Mrs Coombes, who was also a widow of more than two years and owned number 18, was the sister Mrs Morton. It seems that the two women had been drawn closer together because of their unfortunate widowhood status and as a consequence the childless Mrs Coombes had convinced her sister and niece to come and live with her. And even though Arthur had been momentarily moved when hearing this flow of tittle-tattle across the counter of the post office, his stoic resolve of never allowing his emotions to even break surface for an instant, resulted in him speedily making an unobtrusive exit as more urgent thoughts thrust there way forward for his attention.

However, almost three months were to pass by with Arthur patiently managing to maintain his quiet and respectable manner whilst carefully concealing his finely thought out double identity ruse of being himself, the dutiful provider to the residents of 17 Oakshott Road and of Harold Morris the travelling salesman in Coventry.

Although, it has to be said that it had become a very strange sensation for Arthur to be recognised as Harold Morris when in the vicinity of his Coventry lodgings, especially at the local newsagents and fish and chip shop which he patronised as often as possible. In both those chatter centres he had come to be referred to by name, as Mr Morris which indicated to Arthur that his incognito had clearly been accepted as part of the community, an important factor in his planning.

The truth of the matter was that he had made a concerted effort over the three months or so to nurture this familiarity, for the simple reason being that his plans dictated he acquire a plausible alias to drop into if everything were to go wrong. Even so, the one thing that had allowed Arthur to preserve the facade was the knowledge that all his intricate planning, so simple in its conception had been firmly in place from almost the very beginning, even before the magical manifestation of his sister Charlotte at her graveside. All it had needed was her confirmation for it to come to fruition.

And the day he had chosen to set his plan into motion had been clearly and indelibly branded into his mind. It was to be Monday 28th September 1953, his D Day and Arthur felt no qualms whatsoever, just a cold deliberation of purpose as he had mentally ticked off each day that drew him closer to his Day of Deliverance. Nothing was going to sway him from what he was now considering as a kind of destiny, a fate filled need to rid himself of all the humiliation and degradation that he faced the instant he stepped over the threshold of 17 Oakshott Road.

With this renewed, vengeful rational of thought Arthur had discovered such a guiltless conviction in what he must do, that any possible sense of self condemnation that he may have entertained had been quashed by the knowledge that in all conscience the deadly outcome from all his planning was in fact the right one. And that was to be the total eradication of an evil dynasty in the form of a sadistic and sick minded mother and her equally corrupt daughter. It must be said however, that even though he was fully aware of the diabolical aspect of this final solution, he was now more than ever powerless to halt the festering need in him to see it through to its bitter end.

xi.
Shilling In The Slot

The day when it dawned was exactly one week after the opening of the third shop in Wolverhampton. Arthur had felt an understandable sense of pride as he watched the steady stream of customers entering and the steady stream exiting with their purchases. The sense of pride had extended to the gathering realisation that all three new shops were now open and the signs were that they were going to be a success. This was reflected in a telegram he had received from Mr Soames on the morning after the opening, merely stating just two words 'Well Done!'

And with those few words creating a very rare smile to adorn his face, Arthur had felt that he had more than repaid the trust that Mr Soames had placed in him.

But that was a week ago and past tense now, and he must concentrate totally on what he had to do. And with this motivation firmly fixed in his mind he walked out of 17 Oakshott Road on the fateful Monday morning of 28th September 1953, as usual by 7am, to put his well deliberated plan into operation. And keeping to his usual route and routine he breathed in the clean frosty air of the early autumnal morning with a glowing sense of satisfaction, in the knowledge that everything was now in place and with no turning back.

From there he caught the bus into Birmingham and breakfasted at the little cafe before continuing the short distance to Snow Hill Station to catch the train to Bromsgrove, where he was to spend the day performing his normal regional manager's duties.

The day passed uneventfully with Arthur checking the stock, giving some extra training to the new staff, discussing sales and company policy with the manager, speaking to customers, rearranging the displays and the window dressing. All of which were very normal duties for a person in his position to undertake.

Even so, never far from his mind was what he had set himself to do and no matter how deeply he allowed his mind to dwell on this, he was always aware that he must maintain as normal an appearance as possible. And so by acting perfectly naturally he hoped that no one would notice anything different about him if they were to be questioned later.

But with everything so well thought out there should not be any doubts in his mind that by this time tomorrow he would be free of the debilitating weight of loathing and hatred that was aimed solely at the landlady and her daughter in 17 Oakshott Road. His insurance being, that if anything was to go wrong he had made certain that Arthur Wilmot could disappear without trace and be reborn in the guise of the anonymous Harold Morris the travelling salesman.

Harold Morris, the small man with the greyish brown hair and slightly bushy moustache, the round horn rimmed spectacles, the rather ancient raincoat and the permanently placed trilby hat, who sucked continually on the stem of an unlit old pipe and apart from the similarity in height, the direct antithesis of his creator. And when Arthur had taken the opportunity to glance in a mirror he had been shocked at the transformation and yet the strange part of his assuming this new character was that he felt comfortable with it, for Arthur actually liked Harold.

Closing time came and he watched as the staff methodically went through the end of the day routine. And saying his 'Good nights' he made his way to the Bromsgrove railway station and arrived back at Snow Hill at a quarter to seven. There he had a cheese and onion sandwich and a pot of tea in the Refreshment Rooms on Platform 7, all very normal practice for him before taking his usual place on the bench outside for an hour or so, merely to watch all the passersby and to once again imagine the worlds they might live in.

He returned to Oakshott Road later than normal, just after ten thirty and crept as silently as possible to his room at the back of the house, pausing only twice to listen at the bedroom doors of the sleeping Beatrice and then her mother. And in each case he could tell by the various nasal snorts and grunts that emanated from within each room that both were well asleep.

And then he was into the welcome solitude of his own room, to wait, for it would be six hours before he could make his next move and now should be the time when his vigil through the dark hours should evoke recriminations from his conscience. But it was a practiced art with Arthur that his conscience was a dormant facility that he could control without any effort. In fact he had spoken silently and at length with his sister only the day before, when he had visited her grave and she had again confirmed that what he intended to do was the correct course of action to relieve this heavy burden of vengeful hatred that he was carrying.

So sitting thoughtfully in his one armchair and staring out at the black night sky through his window he reached into his jacket's inside pocket for his wallet and took out the small leather envelope and once again he found the comfort he was seeking by lightly fingering his sister's auburn lock of hair. Slowly he allowed all the distressing thoughts and images that his head had been crowded out by over the previous months to slip into the mists of oblivion and to be replaced by warm, comforting images of his sister Charlotte and then by those of little Amy, their smiles dissolving any slight remnants of apprehension that might still have had a place in his mind.

He then began to sense that he was drifting gently through a foggy haze with more pleasant reminiscences of his mother and father appearing before him, smiling the gentle smiles that he had so often sought comfort in all those years before, smiles that he now looked on to glean a kind of approval from, for what he was intending to do in just a few hours time. And it was those so clearly remembered smiles and the implied approval that they now seemed to be giving, and the cherished warmth that emanated from Charlotte and even little Amy that were the last, conscious impressions that Arthur saw as he slipped into something not quite deep sleep but rather resembling a state of dreamless suspended animation.

And he was still in exactly the same position when he opened his eyes after some inner instinct had alerted his mind back to reality. Glancing at the hands of his alarm clock he was able to confirm the time to be a quarter to five, the precise time that he had planned on. Slowly, almost nonchalantly he stood and stretched and replaced the small leather envelope with the precious strands of auburn hair, back into his wallet.

Moving very quietly around the room he made sure that it looked as if he had spent a normal night asleep in it. Then running the palm of his hand over his chin he found comfort in his decision not to use the bathroom to wash and shave, simply because the noise would certainly have alerted Mrs Ansell at this early hour. But the truth of the matter was, because of his fair complexion and boyish countenance Arthur found that on occasions he only needed to shave every two days, it was purely pride that usually made him drag his razor over his hairless chin every morning.

However, this morning he paused momentarily to examine the face that appeared in his mirror as he made for the door. He lightly flicked his fine wispy fair hair into place, that even from his early twenties had never totally covered his shiny scalp and then his gaze took in the round, almost flawless face and deep, dark eyes that seemed to hold a myriad of secrets behind them. For a long moment he contemplated the image and then with a contented smirk and a straightening of his collar and tie he thought to himself, how different he was to Harold Morris.

So now fully committed, he picked up his raincoat and trilby hat and the black leather brief case that Mr Soames had presented him with on his appointment to Regional Manager. Then very stealthily he left his room to make his way along the landing, stopping only to listen at each of the two doors of his landlady and her daughter's rooms to confirm that the occupants were still asleep. Silently making his way down stairs, he avoided the centre of each step so as not to induce some uncalled for creaking until finally he reached the hallway. From there it was along past the front sitting room door and its ever present taint of stale tobacco smoke and then to the rear parlour door and finally the kitchen and the scullery.

Now was the moment to put the most important part of his plan into effect. It was the habit, since he had been providing the coins for the gas meter, for both Mrs Ansell and Beatrice to sleep with their gas fires on in their rooms, and with the distinct chilliness creeping into the early mornings Arthur was convinced the fires would be lit. But then, the thought fleetingly scurried across his mind of what if, by some remote chance he was to be thwarted on this occasion and the fires were not lit. And yet as quickly as this instance of uncertainty had entered his head it was replaced by the confident assurance, drawn from his well thought through planning, that the gas fires would be lit. And he was equally certain that they would invariably remain lit well into the morning, which in itself was one small luxury he had deprived himself of when it had been made very plain to him that it was his responsibility to pay for the gas fires to be installed in the first place.

Nevertheless, with a coldness of purpose Arthur opened the pantry door and switched on the light. There in front of him was the gas meter and the isolator tap and in the dismal light he could just make out the miniscule movement of the dial, indicating that gas was flowing up into the rooms above. Quickly he decided there was only just enough on the meter to provide gas until the morning and so to make absolutely sure he pushed a shilling into the slot and turning the key, he heard the coin drop into the box. After all, he thought with a grim glint in his eyes, as it was he who provided the coins to feed the hungry gas meter, on this occasion he was not going to begrudge one more to make sure the gas was flowing unabated to the fires of his landlady and her daughter.

A chill now crept from between Arthur's shoulders and down his spine causing him to remain motionless, frozen to the spot as his attention became transfixed by the dial on the gas meter. For some reason he seemed powerless to free himself from his hypnotic gaze, but it was not a sense of guilt or remorse which now stayed his hand from taking the next fateful step in his plan. No, it was the sudden influx of grinding instances of humiliation and wounding abuse that now seemed to crowd into his head. All the sneering and sniggering and devious manipulating of his vulnerable honesty and good nature that he had suffered ever since he had stepped over the threshold of this abominable house and into the wicked clutches of the malicious Mrs Ansell and her daughter, which had now brought him to this dreadful and final conclusive act of vengeance on his part.

And as the momentary cold blast of disturbing recollections finally began to subside there was, most certainly no sense of guilt or remorse in any part of Arthur's well guarded conscience. No, there was now only calm and a complete sense of measured and unequivocal purpose.

Very slowly he placed his handkerchief over his fingers and turned the stiff isolator tap to the off position, thus shutting down the supply into the house. Raising his head slightly he could almost visualize the two rooms of Mrs Ansell and Beatrice above him, where the gas fire bars would be losing their orange glow as the flickering blue flames diminished before going out completely.

Arthur stood silently listening for almost two minutes to make sure there were no sounds of disturbed movement from above. But all was quiet and so he then proceeded to turn the tap on again, thus allowing the deadly gas back into the house and from there into the rooms of his evil minded tormentors. He felt nothing whatsoever as he made this calculated action, for the cold emotionless, unsentimental resolve that had governed his whole existence had now come fully to the fore. Again he listened and imagined that he could actually hear the almost imperceptible hissing that would be the only warning that gas was now entering the rooms.

Carefully he took his handkerchief and wiped all the areas his fingers had touched. This was a necessary precaution, in that he was not supposed to have had access to this part of the house. Then closing the pantry door quietly, he moved very cautiously towards the back door and pulling it locked behind him, he slipped away into the early morning darkness with an enormous sense of satisfaction that his simple plan had been well executed.

A little under an hour later, after catching the early bus Arthur found himself once again on the bench outside the Refreshment Rooms on Platform 7 of Snow Hill Station, where with a deep reflective sigh he sat very quietly thinking his thoughts of what was done and nothing could change that now, even if he had wanted it to be changed. But deep down he knew that he did not want it to be changed, for now there was just a marauding iciness to his reasoning that in some strange way felt natural to him and not a little exhilarating.

If Arthur was to be honest, the rest of his day at the new Wolverhampton branch was carried out in a kind of daze like state, although on several occasions he did briefly wonder if his plan had been successful and that when he returned to Oakshott Road in the evening he would be forever free of that hellish pair of villainous, grasping abusers. But because that notion had a certain pervasive nature to it he had to be constantly aware of maintaining his normal, methodical and formal approach. Even so, not once did his thoughts indicate the merest glimmer of regret to any of his actions.

Arthur still had the ability to detach himself completely from any emotional dependency in any given situation. That is why he had been able to survive the travesty of the horrors that had been laid before him during his war service years. Where others had buckled under the stresses of what they were seeing and hearing he was able to maintain a staunch and forthright approach that had been well respected by his colleagues and his superiors alike, resulting in his commanding officer's personal commendation. But even that had now gone to the church jumble sale within the pages of one of his Railway albums.

No, there was no remorse or contrition, not even a flickering of guilt. And at the end of a very long day for Arthur, he had to finally admit to himself that he had very little memory of any specific part of it. For with his thoughts being mostly in a self imposed robotic state he had been content to go about his own duties in his normal quiet but authoritative manner and to observe the smooth running of the shop without any interference from him.

And as the branch manager Mr Webber turned the key on his shop door, Arthur was able to wish him a 'good evening' and stroll down to Wolverhampton station with something of an air of the unreal, a sense of not of this world, of somewhere else entirely opposed to where his mind actually was.

Even as his train made its final approach into Snow Hill Station and as he pulled back to avoid the passengers already crowding the corridor in anticipation of a quick exit, he felt no trepidation, no anxiety, so sure was he that what he had done had been the right and correct thing to do. And finally with a cranking and a heavy chuffing from the engine the train came to a stuttering halt with Arthur being one of the last off.

He stood for a few moments to check he had his brief case, raincoat and trilby hat and also his ticket before sauntering, in a quite composed manner towards the underpass that connected the platform he was on to the haven of Platform 7 and the bench outside the Refreshment Rooms.

But as he reached the top of the steps that finally opened out onto Platform 7 the shouted words of a newspaper vendor brought him to an abrupt, quivering halt. At first he was baffled and then disbelieving at what he was actually hearing, which caused him to rub his face furiously in an effort to alert his sluggish senses. That was until the truth of the words finally seeped through and pounded like heavy claps of thunder inside his brain. He stumbled and found the metal handrail to support him as again the vendor's words rang out like some kind of death knell in Arthur's head. Finding the strength within his trembling muscles he staggered up the remaining few steps like a man too fond of the demon drink.

"Extra! Extra! Read all about it!" the vendor cried out announcing the day's headlines. "Five dead in Selly Park gas explosion. Read all about it!"

With his whole body shivering uncontrollably and with a weakness creeping into his legs Arthur continued to seek support against the wall at the top of the steps. But now he could feel the perspiration beginning to trickle down his spine, which contradicted the chill he could feel running through his veins. And for the first time that he could ever remember he felt afraid, not at his actions against his evil minded landlady and her daughter, because that is what he had planned on, but the fear was stimulated purely by the headlines that stated it was a gas explosion, which is not what he had planned on.

With his mind reeling he tried to piece together what could have gone wrong and what had really happened, when his damning thoughts were interrupted.

"Are you alright mate?" the news vendor was asking. "You don't look well!"

Arthur grunted a reply of sorts and pushed himself away from the wall that was supporting him. He delved deep into his trouser pocket and drew out a fist full of coins which he thrust into the vendor's open hand before snatching a copy of the paper and stumbling away to the sanctuary of the bench outside the Refreshment Rooms.

It took more than fifteen minutes for Arthur to collect his jangling thoughts and before he could bring himself to confront the item in the newspaper, for this was a new sensation for Arthur the "ice man" as his RAMC colleagues had known him as. Now all the sadness and sorrow that had been carried and secreted away inside this solitary man all the years of his life were beginning to flow from him in a gushing tide of unremitting anguish and despair. Never before had he felt such a sense of complete and utter desolation. He had planned and prepared himself of being rid of the two she devils from 17 Oakshott Road but the newspaper vendor had declared that five had died and that was the knife that was now burrowing deep into his vulnerable soul. The soul, that by his actions he had hoped to cleanse.

Finally, and with great effort he managed to straighten his back and isolate the small paragraph on the front page. It was only a short piece under the late news column but it described a large, early morning gas explosion in Oakshott Road, Selly Park and the resulting fire had devastated that house and the one adjoining it. It had been confirmed that the five occupants of both houses were dead.

The final few words of the column however, were the words that brought Arthurs mind streaking back to reality with a fearsome clarity, for they announced that the police wished to talk to a third occupant of number 17, who was missing.

"They will be looking for me!" Arthur immediately thought.

A brief statement but with all the connotations of the police suspecting that it was not an accident and knowing exactly who it was to blame. And even now in Arthur's mind he could visualise what had actually occurred, his landlady in a semi soporific state and with her constant need to suppress her addiction for nicotine had lit a match, and that was that. Although this was now a detail that Arthur had unfortunately and tragically overlooked, for his plan had been for Mrs Ansell and Beatrice to succumb quietly in their sleep to the effects of the gas and for it to merely be viewed as a terrible accident.

Now an even colder chill suddenly engulfed him when he considered the other victims of his actions, the occupants of the adjoining semi, number 18 and this would include little Amy, her mother and her aunt. But it was the face of little Amy, that shining little angel with the auburn locks that was blanking out any other thoughts in his throbbing brain and he had snuffed out that tiny light as if it was nothing more than a flickering candle. And even as this thought plagued his mind the delicate features of his sister Charlotte slowly filtered into the picture and with it came the damning thought that in killing the totally innocent little Amy, his sister had also died, all over again. And it was this self confirmed indictment that was now condemning his soul beyond the reaches of any possibility of cleansing or even forgiveness or pardon.

Never before had Arthur been able to show emotion by the shedding of tears but now he sensed a distinct moistness in his eyes, which then emerged into one single tear that clung desperately to his eye lid as if it was reluctant to let go. But using the back of his hand he testily swept the miscreant tear away and merely sat in a brooding silence as the mingling, hazy world of Platform 7 went about its business completely unnoticed by him.

For now all sights and sounds and smells of this most precious of places meant nothing to Arthur, for his mind was a total void of any outside impressions that attempted to interfere with his utter sense of desperation. Only the sweet smiling faces and the long auburn locks of little Amy and his beloved sister Charlotte were all that seemed to occupy and taunt Arthur's shell shocked state of mind. And even as he continued to see them, there in his head, the two smiling faces seemed to merge and fuse into one beautiful picture that left Arthur swooning slightly from the sheer joy the vision was giving him. But then the smiling, tender features began to age and to fade and the hair began to lose its lustre and darken, as the whole image of Amy and Charlotte seemed to shimmer and then finally dissolve completely from his mind.

"I killed them!" Arthur muttered breathlessly to himself. "I...I killed them both!"

And even as the words left his mouth he realised that he was denouncing and damning himself to hell.

"I did!......... I killed them!" he stammered. "I could not kill the one ....without killing the other .....Be...because they are one!......They...are...one!.......and I killed them!....I killed them both!....But..... I didn't mean to!....I....I didn't mean to!"

A dark impenetrable cloud now filled Arthur's mind so that the heavy weight of his groaning conscience tugged hard at his pounding heart, a pounding heart that reverberated in his ears and in his eyes and the sides of his head. So much so that he felt he would scream out, simply to try and relieve the anguish and pain that it was causing him. And within that torture he began to feel the strangest of sensations, as if his fortress of iron resolve was beginning to crumble and to give way to a massive emotional release, a sensation that even now he was inwardly resisting and fighting.

And yet, the fact must be faced that after so many years of holding back, dam like on his emotions, something was bound to give. It was as if Arthur had merely been waiting for the moment that would move him and shake him so severely as to cause the floodgates to be breached and to release all of his carefully filtered and suppressed, deep seated emotions in one overwhelming torrent.

It began with one convulsive, sharp intake of breath, a gasp that was the forerunner of an outpouring of sobbing from a lifetime in which Arthur had never allowed himself to express any form of impassioned reaction before. All those times in the past when he had wanted, had needed to share his grief and sadness with the world but had scrupulously bottled up any outward displays and secreted them away behind his well constructed, ice cold facade.

And the sobbing continued unabated, deep heart wrenching sobbing and tears, tears that flowed in an unrelenting deluge from reddening eyes and down flushed cheeks, yet still concealed behind hands that trembled with each jolt and seizure of the tightly hunched shoulders of this broken, sad little man. And all the while totally oblivious of the probing looks of the passersby.

How long Arthur remained on that bench in that stupor like state of self pity he could not say. He only knew that the crowds that had occupied the platform with the homeward rush had now thinned and there was a more relaxed atmosphere that always seemed to come as the evening progressed.

Arthur was now able to ease the tension in his aching neck and shoulder muscles as he leant back on his bench with a sense of being absolutely drained of any kind of feeling whatsoever. He allowed his head to fall back against the wall of the Refreshment Rooms as his gaze wandered absently around and between the metal beams and glass of the station roof. His mind began to mull over the new developments that had upset his so careful planning, for now he was once more in control and able dissect his thoughts and any decisions that had to be made. All the searing hatred and loathing for his contemptible, evil minded and avaricious landlady and her daughter that he had carried for so long was no more and in its place was merely an enormous sense of burning remorse for the consequences of his vengeful actions.

He would not run and he would not hide, this he was quickly decided upon. But with that decision there was only one alternative and that was to hand himself over to the full impact of the law, which would mean being committed to a madhouse or more likely ending up on the gallows. However, either way was not an option for Arthur, for in his ice cold, resolute manner he had come to the conclusion that he could not live with the unbearable sense of guilt that was even now bubbling like a lava flow ready to spew forth and totally consume him. All the careful preparations in the event of his plans going wrong with his creation of Harold Morris were still in place and open to him, but nothing he had planned allowed for what had now happened by his hand. The whole purpose of his plotting was to avenge himself and be free of his landlady and her daughter, and the gas should have been enough to see that part of his plan succeed but for Mrs Ansell's addiction to nicotine. Silently he cursed her name and damned her to hell.

Arthur sat with his mind completely at ease and his thinking as ever was very rational and logical with regard to his decision making and what he must do. With a long, purposeful intake of breath he dipped into his leather brief case and pulled out the note book and pencil that he always carried and quite deliberately began to write. And what he wrote was nothing less than a complete and detailed confession of his actions, all the intricate planning and what he had hoped to achieve and the reasons for taking such dire actions. The final paragraph confirmed, without referring to them other than his landlady and her daughter, who his intended victims were to have been and how regretful he was that three others had also died. Then tearing the pages from the book, he folded and placed them carefully into his wallet.

And yet, even as he did so he became aware that he was being watched and carefully scrutinized by a railway police officer who was standing at the bottom of the broad flight of steps that led down from the platform connecting bridge some fifty or so yards to his left.

How long he had been there Arthur could not be sure, simply because he had been so involved in what he had been writing. But now with something of a deep sigh of fatalism, Arthur endeavoured to come to terms with the shocking realisation that an accurate description of himself would most certainly have been circulated and it would only have been a matter of time before he was recognised.

For almost half a minute the police officer remained with his whole attention directed towards the small, insignificant man seated on the bench outside the Refreshment Rooms. Then turning, he quickly made his way back up the steps and disappeared from sight along the bridge as he headed towards the main concourse. Instantly Arthur knew he only had minutes, for the officer would soon be in one of the telephone boxes in the booking hall, phoning in his sighting and asking for instructions.

Arthur's eyes remained fixed on the flight of steps as any last instinct to flee from the bench, his sanctuary, diminished in a flash, for nothing he could do or say now would lessen the profound sense of guilt he was feeling over the death of little Amy. A sudden icy shudder passed through the whole of his body as if 'someone had walked over his grave' and in that instant he had a clear understanding that the all consuming sense of damning self-reproach he could feel within him would ultimately be the cross he must carry to Calvary. He could even hear his mother Iris, so many years before teaching him about those very words in one of her Sunday School classes.

"We all have our crosses to bear," she had said, "but you measure the weight of that cross by the guilt you hold in your heart."

And as Arthur thought back over that part of his upbringing and the moral values his mother had instilled into her son through her words and actions, a billowing cloud of blinding shame began to infiltrate into Arthurs mind, which only added to the now unbearable sense of deep remorse that was eating into him with every breath that he took.

Arthur did not move, he had no need to for he was in the place that had been his port of solace during the whole of his troubled life. But this time it was not to merely observe all the comings and goings of his little piece of heaven, this time he was waiting, waiting for the unplanned conclusion to all his scheming and plotting, waiting simply for the end to come and yet regretfully it was not to be with his soul cleansed, rather with it damned and lost for all time.

He looked at the platform clock and saw that it was indicating eight forty three.

From his wallet he drew out the small leather envelope with the lock of auburn hair. For the first time since he had placed it in the envelope he actually removed the delicate strands and looked on them with a tremendous easing of his conscience. Lifting the curling auburn lock to his nose he sniffed at it with almost a sense of ecstasy, believing that he could still detect the faint aroma of his sister that was indelibly imprinted in his memory. He sighed a deep sigh of infinite relief, for he now knew he was to be reunited with his beloved Charlotte, the sister who had looked over him all these years and the sister that at every turn of his life he had spoken to through those few strands of auburn hair. Once again they provided the peace and comfort that he now needed more than ever before, just to see him through the next few minutes. The auburn lock of hair of his sister Charlotte, the sister that only a short time before had spoken to him from beside her own grave.....

"I will be waiting for you," she had whispered.

The words once again rang so meaningfully in his mind.

Now with a real sense of purpose Arthur Wilmot pushed himself to his feet and with the lock of hair still between his fingers he took one more last look around at the so familiar features of this edifice, this monument to mans ingenuity and enterprise. And as he did so he was thankful for the enormous part that the bench outside the Refreshment Rooms on Platform 7 of Snow Hill Station had played in his life.

For a few more seconds he continued to stand there absorbing every fine nuance that this cherished citadel to the power of steam had to offer. And then, still gently fingering those so precious auburn fibres, he slowly moved towards the edge of the platform, somehow avoiding minor collisions with the scattering of faceless figures.

Then standing on the edge of the platform such a peaceful, serene feeling began to fill his whole being to such an extent that he could physically sense the thrill of it. And across the rails on the opposite platform he could see a slender figure in a flowery dress and long auburn locks caressing her shoulders.

Instantly, he recognised the figure and breathed just one word. "Charlotte."

He could feel the heavy thumping of his heart as he stared totally captivated by the apparition, who was even now smiling that so warm and welcoming smile as she raised a hand to give a gentle wave.

A sudden awareness came over Arthur and he quickly looked towards the flight of steps that led to the connecting bridge and was just in time to see two rain coated men and the railway police officer suddenly appear. They stood looking round as if not quite sure where their eyes should be searching. And almost at the same time Arthur's ears identified the rumbling clatter and the huffing and puffing of the eight forty six to Paddington approaching the far end of the platform.

Arthurs gaze once more reverted back across the lines and he was relieved to discover that his sister was still there, still smiling in his direction. It was a smile that he easily remembered as being his and his alone. It belonged to no one else but him, Arthur Wilmot.

Then another, smaller figure materialised close to his sister. The figure was also dressed in a flowery dress with long auburn locks and strikingly resembled the image of Charlotte at a much younger age. And even as Arthur looked a smile appeared on little Amy's face as she took hold of his sister's hand. Now the two stood hand in hand smiling across the tracks at Arthur, two perfect images of one entity, one single person at two stages of their brief, short lives, dashed to oblivion by Arthur's own, cursed hand.

But the sound of the train was growing louder and nearer and Arthur could also hear hurried footsteps approaching him. Across the rails on the opposite platform Charlotte was not waving anymore, she was beckoning him, urging him forward, forward to her side. There was now a marked urgency about her motions and Arthur knew what he must do. And reaching out his hand that held the small lock of Charlottes auburn hair, the hair that could glint with gold in the sun light, he gently opened his fingers and watched the strands separate and flutter away into the night air.

And as Arthur stepped willingly towards the outstretched arms of his sister and the slight figure of little Amy, it was the eight forty six through train to Paddington that caught this quiet man and not the representatives of the law.

xii.
End Of The Line

The bench from outside the Refreshment Rooms on Platform 7 of Snow Hill Station Birmingham was sold by auction to an unknown buyer after the final decline and closure of the station in the late 1960s. An ignominious demolition programme of the station followed and was completed by 1977.

Even so, the question has to be asked if the bench gave as much comfort and solace to those who bought it as it had done for a certain sad, quiet but deeply sensitive man throughout the whole of his journey, his odyssey through life.

However, it has also been noted by several respected authorities that a mysterious, diminutive figure in a dark suit and carrying a raincoat and a trilby hat had been seen on many occasions seated on that very bench in the early hours of the morning, right up until the bench was finally removed after closure......Was it a lost soul seeking redemption perhaps!

I wonder!

****

'Making Notes'...sketched by the authors grandfather on Snow Hill Station October 1951.

By the author.

Beneath The Fickle Moon
    Xlibris   www.xlibrispublishing.co.uk.
The Ballad Of Jessie Gray and other stories
    Xlibris   www.xlibrispublishing.co.uk.
Betrayal Of The Trinity Knot
    Xlibris   www.xlibrispublishing.co.uk.
House Of Penitents and other stories
    Xlibris   www.xlibrispublishing.co.uk.

By the author as a singer/songwriter.

Coming Home
    originally on vinyl. Now on CD (DPLO116) and iTunes and Amazon download.
Some Things Seem So Right
    originally on vinyl. Now on CD (DPLO154) and iTunes and Amazon download.
Nothing Comes Easy
    originally on vinyl. Now on CD (AS7/445) and iTunes and Amazon download.
Old Town
    CD (CD1011SBS) and iTunes and Amazon download.
Scenery
    Paper Bubble) vinyl album. Also on CD (Retro 831) and iTunes and Amazon download.
Paper Bubble Complete Compilation/Behind The Scenery
    CD (Retro999/Cherry Red Records) and iTunes and Amazon download.
Some Place To Be Me
    CD (1011297SBS) and iTunes and Amazon download.
More releases to come.

For more information go to....
www.stillbreezemusic.co.uk
www.xlibrispublishing.co.uk
www.briancranesongs.com
Brian Crane Homesite.

Lightning Source UK Ltd.
Milton Keynes UK
UKHW011429290520
364087UK00001B/57